WALKING
WOUNDED

Best wishes,
Willie McIlvanney

WILLIAM McILVANNEY

WALKING WOUNDED

Hodder & Stoughton
LONDON SYDNEY AUCKLAND TORONTO

British Library Cataloguing in Publication Data

McIlvanney, William, *1936–*
  Walking wounded.
  I. Title
  823' 914[F]

ISBN 0-340-26330-X

Published by Hodder and Stoughton,
a division of Hodder and Stoughton Ltd,
Mill Road, Dunton Green, Sevenoaks, Kent TN13 2YA
Editorial Office: 47 Bedford Square, London WC1B 3DP

Photoset by Rowland Phototypesetting Ltd,
Bury St Edmunds, Suffolk

Printed in Great Britain by St Edmundsbury Press Ltd,
Bury St Edmunds, Suffolk

FOR MY FRIENDS

'Come, come. Did we not all start out with
more important matters on our minds?'
A man I think I overheard in a bar.

And so adrift in unknown selves we lie
Abandoned to dark plucks of circumstance,
Not knowing what will come or what we'll do
Or where the tides of sleep will wash us and
Shy from the sculling shapes that feed on mind,
Feel every certainty drift out of reach
And sigh and hold each other, tryst with touch
To share what is not shareable, and know
The jerking terror of time's undertow
And madly try to dream ourselves a beach.

WALKING WOUNDED

I

Waving

Bert Watson had had a busy day. The consignment of
pullovers with the lion rampant on them was behind
schedule. Manufacture of the turtle-neck sweaters was
having to be put back. Sitting in his office, he heard the
looms run down and they seemed to him like his ambition
giving out.

He looked at the litter on his desk and wondered how he
had come to be manacled to these invoices, how many years
he had spent transferring days from the in-tray to the
out-tray. It would be some time yet before he could go
home, but the thought was merely a reflex, no longer carried
any deep regret. Marie would be waiting there with a
detailed report of how much hoovering she had done today
and what the Brussels sprouts cost. Jennifer would be doing
her usual impersonation of a foundling princess who can't
understand how she has come to be unloaded on such a
crass family and Robert, fruit of his loins and heir to his
ulcers, would be playing songs in which the lyrics only
surfaced intermittently and incomprehensibly.

His mind dwelt on the still sheen of silence from the
factory, played with it briefly, chased it with fancies. The
men and women would be packing up, raucous and ribald.
There would be jocular assignations, male threats of dire
sexual damage to be done and female mockery of the capacity to carry out the threats. There would be visits to the

pub by some before they went home. There would be noisy family meals, clean clothes donned, nights out. There would be unexpected things to happen. For him there were more invoices, roast beef since it was Friday, and News at Ten.

Sally Galbraith knocked at the door and looked in. She waited until his attention returned from contemplation of his own headstone. Her breasts were neatly framed in the doorway, an idyllic scene observed from an express train.

'It's Duncan MacFarlane again,' she said.

'Just now, Sally?'

'Third time today, Mr Watson.' Her expression was a plea on behalf of Duncan. Bert Watson could understand it. He liked Duncan too. Most people did. 'And it's the fourth day this week he's asked to see you.'

'You know what it's about?'

'Personal. But it must be important.'

'I give in,' Bert Watson said and nodded.

He was working on a form when Duncan came in. It was a few moments before he glanced up and saw Duncan standing there, awkwardly. Duncan must have been about twenty but he wore his years lightly. Bert Watson knew that Duncan's father was dead and that he lived with his mother. He wondered if that early bereavement was what had given Duncan his aura of unselfconscious vulnerability, made women want to mother him and men want to give him fatherly advice.

'Have a seat, Duncan. With you in a minute.'

The invoice couldn't be right. How did two dozen dresses, which were the most expensive item they had, cost less than two dozen women's sweaters?

'Yes, Duncan. What can I do for ye?'

'What it is, Mr Watson,' Duncan said. 'Ah'd like a loan of five hundred pounds and three months' leave of absence.'

Perhaps it was the number of items that was wrong. It depended which one of those two entries was right, if either.

'Yes, Duncan. You were saying?'

'Ah'd like a loan of five hundred pounds and three months' leave of absence.'

The cost of the sweaters was correct. Bert Watson looked up. Duncan's blue eyes were staring at him steadily. Their quiet patience defied Bert Watson to hear what he had heard. He glanced at his watch, not sure whether he was checking the hour or the date or the fact that time still functioned.

'I can't have heard what I thought I heard, Duncan,' he said. 'Come again.'

'I was just wondering,' Duncan said. He paused and chewed his lip. 'If I could have a loan of four hundred pounds and three months' leave of absence.'

Bert Watson looked at the Pirelli calendar on his wall. Samantha, her see through blouse wet from the sea, appeared to be pouting more outrageously than ever. She couldn't believe Duncan either. It occurred irrelevantly to Bert Watson that she was dressed very inappropriately for March.

'*Four* hundred pounds?' Bert Watson said, as if by interviewing the incredible you could get it to make sense. 'I thought you said five hundred pounds at first.'

'Well, yes. Ah did.'

'What made you change your mind, then?'

'Well, it's maybe a bit much,' Duncan said.

'That's certainly one way of looking at it,' Bert Watson said.

'Mind you,' Duncan said with the air of a man anxious that the scale of his needs shouldn't be underestimated. 'That's really what Ah need. Five hundred pounds is just the bare minimum. But Ah would settle for four hundred. Ah mean, Ah can understand your situation as well.'

'Thanks, Duncan.'

Both sat letting the generosity of Duncan's self-denial sink in. Bert Watson's eyes strayed towards Samantha again, as they often did.

'So,' he said, looking back at Duncan and finding him

not much less exotic than Samantha. 'Let's see. You want four hundred pounds. Right? You're sure that's the final figure?' Duncan hesitated briefly before nodding. 'Four hundred then. And you also want three months' leave of absence. There's nothing you'd like to add to that? Like a magnum of champagne?'

Duncan smiled at the preposterousness of Bert Watson's suggestion.

'Duncan,' Bert Watson said. 'I hope you won't think me nosey or carping. But who's supposed to give you this money? I mean, you're asking *me* to give you four hundred pounds?'

'Well, Ah was thinkin' of the firm, really. Through you, like. You're the head man. Ah mean, Ah've worked here since Ah left the school.'

'What age are you now, Duncan?'

'Nineteen.'

'Uh-huh. It's a wee bit early for a golden handshake, is it not?'

Duncan was mildly outraged.

'Oh no,' he said. 'Nothin' like that. Ah said "a loan".'

'So you did, right enough.'

'Ah would pay it back, obviously.'

'How?'

'Off ma wages, like. When Ah come back to work.'

'Duncan. That's a bit of money. You would just about make it before your pension's due.'

'Ah've worked it out,' Duncan said. 'Say, a tenner a week. Do it inside a year.'

'Uh-huh. As long as the malnutrition doesn't keep you off your work.'

'Sorry?'

'Duncan, are you in trouble?'

Duncan was mystified.

'Trouble?'

'Why do you need this money and the leave of absence?'

'You mean you don't know?'

'Duncan. I'm asking you.'

Duncan smiled in wonder at Bert Watson's innocence.

'Argentina,' he said.

Bert Watson checked with Samantha again and it was as if her upraised arm was pointing to the year above her head: 1978. He understood. Duncan came into more or less normal focus again. He wasn't mad. At least he wasn't mad in the eccentric way that Bert Watson had been beginning to imagine. He was mad with a natural madness. Bert Watson looked at Duncan and smiled. Duncan smiled back. Bert Watson shook his head and looked at his desk and smiled again.

It was interesting to have in his office the first case he had known personally of the lunacy that was sweeping the country. For weeks he had been aware of the terrible grip the disease had been taking on Scotland, like a mental Bubonic. Everybody wanted to go to Argentina. Men were apparently standing up suddenly in perfectly peaceful houses and announcing to their families, as if seized by strange messages from the air, 'I want to go to Argentina'. More than that, some of them were trying to fulfil the urge. Every other day, in newspapers or on television, new stories came of wild plans being hatched about how to get there. Rowing boats had been mentioned. Two men from Tarbert, Loch Fyne, were rumoured to be cycling. A bookmaker from the east was said to be hiring a submarine. Since the Scottish football team had qualified for the World Cup Finals to be held in Argentina, a one-directional wanderlust had become the national insanity. Bert Watson smiled again.

'You want to go to Argentina?'

'Don't you?'

Duncan's astonishment struck home. Bert Watson did, or at least he had thought about how good it would be to go. He had caught an early, if mild, form of the fever. He had daydreamed of taking his holidays early, of joining in the triumphant entry of the Scots into Buenos Aires for the final stages of the competition. But Marie's hatred of football had been a swiftly effective antidote. She wouldn't have considered it and he could never have matched the chauvinist brutality of a friend of his who, having dreamed for twelve years of the only holiday he had ever really wanted to take, came in one day and announced to his wife, 'I've fixed the holidays'.

'I've always wanted you to surprise me like that,' she said. 'Where are we going?'

'You're going to Pontin's Holiday Camp with the kids,' he had said. 'And I'm going to East Africa on safari.'

Bert Watson had cured himself without ever mentioning it to Marie. His only active concession to the mania around him had been the line they were doing in lion rampant pullovers. Everybody else was cashing in, with flags and scarves and wall-posters. Why shouldn't he? The pullovers were doing well. That was something. You have to be sensible, he thought, as he looked at Duncan.

'How would you be going to get there, Duncan?' he asked.

'Through America,' Duncan replied crisply.

'Through America? How do you mean?'

'Go to New York first. Then right through America.'

Duncan referred to it like a main street.

'But America doesn't border Argentina, Duncan. That still leaves you with a certain distance to go.'

'What? You mean Central America and that? Oh yes.'

'And South America. Argentina's quite well down the map.'

'That's right.'

'You're talking about 7,000 miles.' Abandoned dreams have their uses.

'As much as that?'

Duncan pursed his lips and nodded. He looked as if he might be wondering whether to take another five pounds with him.

'7,000 miles. You ever been out of the country?'

'Blackpool,' Duncan said. Then he added significantly, 'Twice.'

'Blackpool in England?'

'Is there another, like?'

'I don't know, Duncan. I just wondered. But that's all?'

'Well, with my mother and that, I don't get about much.'

'Sounds as if you'd like to make up for it. You would go overland then?'

'That's it. America, Central America. The lot.'

'You heard of the Darien Gap?'

'The what?'

'It's jungle. In Panama. There's no means of transport there.'

'Bound to be something.

'Uh-huh. Who would you be going with?'

'Well, Danny Wright would like to go. If he can get away.'

'Who's Danny Wright?'

'He's a mate of mine. Well, not a mate really. But Ah know him. He's keen to go.'

'He from Graithnock, too?'

'Originally. But he works in Coventry now. We've been on the phone a lot. We would meet up in London. Heathrow Airport.'

'And what about Danny Wright?'

'What about him?'

'Has he been abroad much?'

'He's been on holiday to Spain. But he's not absolutely sure yet.'

'You mean you might go yourself?'

'See how it turns out.'

Samantha's shock was growing. Her eyes, among other things, were popping. Bert Watson thought of Duncan's dead father. He had a vague image of a grave in turmoil. He remembered a Latin phrase from school:*in loco parentis*.

'Duncan,' he said. 'This is a hosiery, not the Clydesdale Bank. Be fair. How can I do this? I'm just the manager here. Mary Simmons is talking about wanting a fur coat. Jackie Stevens was telling me he fancies a different car. Am I supposed to advance them the money as well?'

'But this is a special case,' Duncan said.

'Special case? Every man and boy and most of the women in Scotland would like to go.' Except Marie, he thought. 'Be fair, Duncan, it can't be done.'

'Ah mean it's not every year we're in the Finals of the World Cup.'

'I'm beginning to think it's a good thing. It can't be done, Duncan. It's a daft idea. Anyway, we can't spare you from the factory for three months. We've got our summer lines to get out.'

Duncan thought about it.

'That's it?'

'That's it, Duncan.'

Bert Watson felt sorry for Duncan and glad at the same time. He was saving him from himself. Somewhere the subsoil settled in a peaceful grave.

'Well, thanks for talkin' about it anyway.'

Duncan stood up.

'No problem, Duncan. You can see it all on the telly, anyway. Probably get a better view.'

The price on the sweaters was right. That meant the error was in calculating the cost of two dozen woollen dresses.

'Ah'll let ye know when Ah'm givin' in ma week's notice.'

When Bert Watson looked up, Duncan was on his way to the door.

'Duncan! What did you say?'

'Ah'm not sure exactly when Ah'll be packin' up. See, Ah've got to try an' make as much money as possible. An' Ah've got to give maself time to get there. Could take six or seven weeks, they reckon.'

'You pack up your job, that's it.'

'Ach, well.'

'Duncan! Don't do this.'

He came out from behind his desk.

'Ah've got to.'

'Duncan. Listen. Take another few weeks to think about it.'

'Ah've thought about it for months.'

'What about money?'

'Ah've been savin' up for four year.'

'How much?'

'Ah've got over a thousand. But Ah'm leavin' half for ma maw. So she's all right.'

'Four years? How did you know we would qualify for the Finals?'

'Ah just knew.'

Bert Watson felt awe. He stared into the impenetrable blueness of Duncan's eyes and knew they were as far from his control as Argentina. No wonder Sally's face and the face of just about every woman in the place softened a little whenever Duncan's name was mentioned. Christ, Bert Watson thought, I think I feel the same about him myself.

Here was a boy who didn't know South America from another planet. His knowledge of the world wouldn't have covered a lapel badge. But he was preparing to travel 7,000 miles on a few hundred pounds to watch a football team. And he was going. The eyes allowed of no alternative. If you couldn't help him, he understood. But he was still going.

Bert Watson remembered that Duncan's father had been a first division football player. That and the fact that Duncan was leaving money for his mother finished Bert Watson. He felt the injustice of being confronted by an innocence as brave as Duncan's. He briefly tried to muster sensible arguments in his mind – the need to keep a job, the hazards of the trip, the importance of career. But he wasn't hypocritical enough to let them reach his mouth. Duncan was right. Who needs a career? It was never any substitute for a life.

He stared at Duncan and envied him his eyes. He wondered where they were going, what they would see. He looked past Duncan wistfully, as if straining to hear something, perhaps an echo of that strange internal music of the young that promises so much. The moment passed and he was left feeling like the boy with the limp the Pied Piper left behind. In place of that lost elation all he had was self-awareness. He understood afresh how the responsibility of status could cripple your enjoyment. He was reminded of the price he paid for career and respectability, a constant drain on his spontaneity he hardly noticed any more, like the tax on tobacco. He saw himself as someone waving to life as it passed by. But if all he could do was wave, he would wave nice. He wasn't so far gone that he would be giving it the V-sign.

'Duncan,' he said. 'If you're going, you're going. Your job'll be here for you when you get back. If you get back. You relax on that score. That's all I can promise. About the money. Let me think about it. No promises there, mind.'

But he was already making a promise to himself. He would be taking a collection for Duncan. He couldn't think of anybody who wouldn't want to give, especially among the women. And he would top it up himself and make sure it was respectable. Marie wouldn't even know about it.

'Mr Watson,' Duncan said. He was shaking his head, the blue eyes even wider. 'That's just great. That is just great. Ah mean . . .'

Duncan stood with his hands out, waiting for the words to arrive that would match his gratitude. His eyes gave out their innocent incandescence, unaware of what an affront they were to Bert Watson's sense of his own life.

'Duncan. I'm busy, right? We'll talk more about this in a day or two.'

Duncan smiled and nodded and turned away vaguely, trying to work out where the door was.

'And Duncan. Don't go on the bevvy tonight to celebrate. You're saving up. Remember?'

Duncan gave the thumbs up and went out. Bert Watson sat down behind his desk. He stared at the door. He remembered an evening with Marie before they were engaged. They had been walking near the Bringan and it started to rain. Sheltering among some trees, they kissed and found lust waiting for them as if by appointment. They got down to it there and then, churning the loam with their bodies, writhing on tree roots and wet leaves, gasping among sensations of dark sky and scuttering noises of animal life and nervously interrupted birdsong. Finished, they waited to come back inside their bodies, their bare thighs frosting in the evening air. The rain had stopped sometime. As they picked the residue of their passion from each other like monkeys grooming, twigs from Marie's hair, small balls of impacted mud from his knees, Bert noticed the ingrained dirt on Marie's thighs and the embedded imprint of a root. The sight thrilled him. It was as if he had won her from the earth itself. His trousers had been ruined with mud, he remembered.

He would have settled for having his trousers in that state now, no matter how much they cost. He wondered what Marie thought of that moment, if she ever thought about it. Perhaps she saw it as the kind of holiday from common sense you could have when you were young and daft, but not any more. Certainly, he couldn't imagine her enjoying the dirt. She had turned herself into a Geiger counter for dust and seemed able to hear a glass making a ring-mark on a table from the next room.

Never mind a blood test before marriage, Bert thought. They should invent a machine that, when you stepped into it, projected your nature into the future so that the other person could see which characteristics would survive, which aspects of your character would wither and which get more pronounced. Then maybe you could tell which randy teenager was destined to become a pillar of the Women's Guild, which demure young woman would learn how to keep a tiger in the bedroom, and which girl who could bare herself beautifully among the trees would, in middle age, wear a nightdress like a cotton chastity belt.

Bert Watson sighed. He sat in his expensive suit, successful, longing for mud. What was the exact miscalculation with the dresses?

'Who gives a monkey's fart?' he said aloud and looked at Samantha and wondered if Sally had left the office yet.

2

Performance

Fast Frankie White didn't go into a bar. He entered. He felt his name precede him like a fanfare he had to live up to. As with a lot of small criminals, he had no house of his own, no money in the bank, no deposit account of social status to draw on. He had no fixed place in the scheme of things that could feed back a clear sense of himself, be a mirror. His only collateral was his reputation, a whiff of mild scandal that clung round him like eau-de-Cologne.

Being an actor, he needed applause. His took the form of mutterings of 'Fast Frankie White' most places he went because he chose to go places where they would mutter it. Without that reminder of who he was, he might forget his lines. His favourite lines were cryptic throwaways that reverberated in the minds of the gullible with vaguely dark potential.

'Been doin' a wee job,' he said.

'Checkin' out a couple of things,' he said.

'A good thing I don't pay income tax.'

'This round's on the Bank of Scotland.'

'He's got his own style, Frankie,' some people said. But that was a less than astutely critical observation. It was really a lot of other people's styles observed from the back row of the pictures, a kind of West of Scotland American. Once, when he was twenty, he had seen a Robert Taylor film about New York where some people were wearing white

suits. He had snapped his fingers and said, 'I'm for there!'
A few weeks later, by a never-explained financial alchemy,
he was. A few weeks later, he was back but he liked to
talk about New York. 'There's half-a-million people in the
Bronx,' he would say. 'And most of them's bandits.' It
wasn't Fodor's Guide to the USA but it sounded impressive,
said quickly. And Frankie said everything quickly.

'The Akimbo Arms' was one of the pubs where he liked to
make his entrance. He was originally from Thornbank, a
village near Graithnock, but he lived in Glasgow now, people
said. Frankie didn't say where he lived. He would simply
appear in a Graithnock bar, dressed, it seemed, in items auc-
tioned off from the wardrobe department of some bankrupt
Hollywood studio and produce a wad of notes.

This time he was wearing a light blue suit, pink shirt,
white tie and grey shoes. He looked as if he had stepped out
of a detergent advert.

'Where's ma sunglasses?' somebody said.

But Frankie was already flicking a casual hand in acknowledgement of people who didn't know who he was. He
walked round to the end of the bar where he could have his
back against the wall, presumably in case the G-men burst
in on him, and he prepared to give his performance.

It was a poor house. Matinées usually were. Mick Haggerty was standing along the bar from him, in earnest
debate with an unsuspecting stranger, who probably hadn't
realised Mick's obsession until it was too late.

'Give me,' Mick was saying, 'the four men that've played
for Scotland an' their names've only got three letters in
them.'

Frankie hoped for the stranger's sake that he didn't get
the answer right. Doing well in one of Mick's casual football
quizzes was a doubtful honour, earning you the right to face
more and more obscure questions the relevance of which to
football wasn't easy to see. 'Tell me,' Frankie had once said
to Mick by way of parody. 'In what Scotland–England

game did it rain for four-and-a-half minutes at half-time? And how wet was the rain?'

Over in the usual corner Gus McPhater was sitting with two cronies. Frankie hated the big words Gus used. That left Big Harry behind the bar, besides three others Frankie didn't know. Big Harry had finally noticed him and was approaching with the speed of a mirage.

'Frankie,' Big Harry said.

'Harry. I'll have a drop of the wine of the country.'

'Whit?'

'A whisky, Harry. Grouse. And what you're havin' yourself?'

Big Harry turned down the corners of his mouth even further. He looked at Frankie as if dismayed at his insensitivity.

'Me?' Big Harry said. 'Ye kiddin'? Wi' ma stomach? Ye want a death on yer conscience? Still.' His face assumed a look of martyred generosity. 'Tell ye what. Ah'll take the price of it an' have it when Ah finish. Probably no' get a wink of sleep the night. But ye've got to get some pleasure.'

Frankie remembered Harry's nickname – Harry Kari. He wasn't sure whether the nickname was because that was what everybody felt like trying after a conversation with Harry or because that was what people thought Harry should do. No wonder Gus McPhater was quoted as saying, 'Harry does for conversation what lumbago does for dancin'.' Harry was the kind of barman who told you *his* problems.

'Religion?' Gus McPhater was saying. He was always saying something. 'Don't waste ma time. The opium of the masses. It's done damage worse than a gross of atomic bombs. Chains for the brainbox, that's religion. Ministers? Press agents for the rulin' classes. Ye'll no' catch me in a church. If Ah could, Ah'd cancel ma christenin' retrospectively. Take yer stained-glass windaes. Whit's a windae for? To see through. Right? So what do they do? They cover it in pictures. So that when ye look at the light. The light, mind ye. That's how ye see, ye know. Light refractin' on yer pupils. When ye look for the light, it gets translated intae what they want ye tae see. How's that for slavery? An' whit d'ye see? A lot of holy mumbo-jumbo. People Ah don't know from Adam. What've a bunch of first-century Jewish fanatics got to do wi' me? Ah'll tell ye what. Know when Ah'll go intae a church? When it's man's house. When the stained-glass windaes are full of holy scenes of rivetters in bunnets and women goin' the messages wi' two weans hangin' on to their arse an' auld folk huddled in at one bar of an electric fire after fifty years o' slavin' their guts out for a society that doesny care if they live or die. Those would be windaes worth lookin' at. That's what art should be. Holy pictures of the people. Or a mosaic even. How about that? See when they made that daft town centre. The new precinct. The instant slum. See instead o' that fountain. Why not a big mosaic? Showin' the lives of the people here an' now. How about that? The Graithnock mosaic. Why no?'

Frankie had no desire to join in. He contented himself with a mime of his superior status. Gus McPhater depressed him. People listened to him as if the noises he made with his mouth meant something. He was a balloon. A lot of stories were told about him. He was supposed to have travelled all round the world. He was supposed to be writing a novel or short stories or something. Frankie didn't believe any of them.

Gus seemed to Frankie an appropriate patron saint for Graithnock. He was like the town itself – over the hill and sitting in dark pubs inventing the past. Frankie could remember this place when the industry was still going strong. There had been some vigour about the place then. They were all losers now – phoneys, like Gus McPhater.

Frankie couldn't believe this place. The only kind of spirit in it was bottled. He felt like an orchid in a cabbage-patch.

Where was the old style, the old working-class gallousness? Since the Tory government had come to power, it had really done a job on them, slaughtering all the major industry. They believed they were as useless as the government had told them they were. These men were the cast-offs of capitalism. They were pathetic.

Well, he was different. If the system was trying to screw him, he would screw it. He had his own heroes and they weren't kings of industry. He thought of McQueen. He wondered how long it would be before McQueen got back out. McQueen, there was a man. He was more free in the nick than most men were outside it.

That was what you had to do: defy your circumstances. You were what you declared yourself to be. Frankie looked round the bar and made a decision. He would buy a drink for someone. He pulled his wad of money from his pocket. In the flourish of the gesture he became a successful criminal.

He decided on Gus McPhater's group. His distaste for them somehow made the gesture grander. He felt like Robin Hood giving the poor a share of his spoils. Besides, Gus was a great talker. Buying him a drink was as good as a photograph in the paper. They would know he had been. He threw a fiver on the counter.

'Harry,' he said loudly. 'Give Gus an' the boys whatever they want.'

He noticed a boy who was drinking alone watching him interestedly. It was all the encouragement Frankie needed. He made an elaborate occasion of getting the drinks and taking them over to Gus's table. He dismissed their thanks with a wave. He took his change and put some of the silver into the bottle where they collected for the old folks. The whole thing became a mini-epic, a Cecil B. De Mille production called 'The Drink'.

'Okay,' Frankie said, saluting the room. 'Don't do anythin' Ah wouldn't do. If ye can think of anythin' Ah wouldn't do.'

As he went out, he heard the boy asking, 'Who *is* that?'

Stepping into the street, he felt the gulped whisky sting his stomach. It was a twinge that matched the bad feeling the pub had given him. Hopeless, he thought. But maybe he was wrong. He remembered the admiration on the boy's face as he had asked who Frankie was. Frankie lightened his step and started to whistle.

A good actor never entirely knows the impact he is having. Perhaps in the thinnest house, unnoticed beyond the glare of the actor's preoccupation, a deep insight is being experienced or young ambitions being formed for life.

He would try 'The Cock and Hen'. There might be some real people in there. He side-stepped into a shop doorway and checked his wad of money. He had three fivers left and he repositioned them carefully to make sure they were concealing the packing of toilet paper inside that made them look like a hundred. He would try 'The Cock and Hen'.

3

On the sidelines

B ritish Summer Time had officially begun but, if you
didn't have a diary, you might not have noticed. The
few people standing around in the Dean Park under a
smirring rain didn't seem to be convinced. They knew the
clocks had been put forward an hour – that was what
enabled these early evening football matches to take place.
But the arbitrary human decision to make the nights lighter
hadn't outwitted the weather. The Scottish climate still had
its stock of rain and frost and cold snaps to be used up
before the summer came, assuming it did.

Two football pitches were in use. On one of them a works'
game was in progress. On the adjoining pitch two Boys'
Brigade teams were playing. Standing between touchlines,
John Hannah, his coat collar up, paid most attention to the
Boys' Brigade game – he was here to see Gary – but the
works' match, so noisy and vigorous and expletive, was
impossible to ignore. It impinged on the comparative de-
corum of the boys' game like the future that was coming to
them, no matter what precepts of behaviour the Company
Leaders tried to impose on them. John had heard some of
the other parents complaining ostentatiously at half-
time about the inadvisability of booking a pitch beside a
works' game. 'After all, it's an organisation to combat
evil influences, not arrange to give them a hearing,' a
woman in a blue antartex coat and jodhpurs and

riding-boots had said. Presumably the horse was a white charger.

John found the contrast between the games instructive. It was like being sandwiched between two parts of his past. The works' game was an echo of his own origins. He had himself played in games like that often enough. Standing so close to the crunch of bone on bone, the thud of bodies, the force of foot striking ball, he remembered what a physically hard game football is. Watching it from a grandstand, as he had so often lately, you saw it bowdlerised a little, refined into an aesthetic of itself. The harshness of it made him wonder if that was why he hadn't pursued the game as determinedly as his talent might have justified. He hoped that wasn't the reason but lately the sense of other failures had made him quest back for some root, one wrong direction taken that had led on to all the others. He had wondered if he had somehow always been a quitter, and his refusal to take football seriously as a career had come back to haunt him.

Three separate people whose opinions he respected had told him he could be a first-class professional footballer. The thought of that had sustained him secretly at different times of depression for years, like an option still open, and it was only fairly recently that he had forced himself to throw away the idea out of embarrassment. He was forty now. For years the vague dream of playing football had been like a man still taking his teddy-bear to bed with him. He might still occasionally mention what had been said to him but, whereas before he had named the three men and sometimes described the games after which they had said it, now the remark had eroded to a self-deprecating joke: 'A man once told me . . . At least I think that's what he said – I couldn't be sure because his guide-dog was barking a lot at the time'. The joke, like a lot of jokes, was a way of controlling loss.

'Oh, well done, Freddie!' the woman in the jodhpurs whinnied.

John supposed that Freddie was her son. The kind of parents who attended these games were inclined to see one player in sharp focus and twenty-one meaningless blurs, as if parenthood had fitted their eyes with special lenses. What Freddie had done was to mis-head the ball straight up into the air so that it fell at the feet of an opponent. It had to be assumed that the expression of admiration that was torn involuntarily from the mouth of Freddie's mother was due to the surprising height, about thirty feet, the ball had achieved by bouncing off Freddie's head. Freddie's mother was apparently not scouting for one of the senior clubs.

Gary, John decided after applying rigorous rules of non-favouritism to his judgment, was playing quite well. At ten, he had already acquired basic ball control and he wasn't quite as guilty as most of them were of simply following the ball wherever it went, as if they were attached to it by ropes of different lengths. John had been following Gary's games religiously all season, as a way of showing him that he was still very much involved in his life though he might not live in the same house, and the matches had acquired the poignancy of a weekly recital for John, a strange orches-tration of his past and his present and his uncertain future.

The movingness was an interweave of many things. Part of it was memory. A municipal football park in Scotland is a casually haunted place, a grid of highly sensitised earth that is ghosted by urgent treble voices and lost energy and small, fierce dreams. John's dreams had flickered for years most intensely in such places. He could never stand for long watching Gary and these other boys without a lost, wandering pang from those times finding a brief home in him. On countless winter mornings he had stood beside parks like this and remembered his own childhood commit-ment and wondered what had made so many Scottish boys so desperate to play this game. He could understand the physical joy of children playing football in a country like Brazil. But on a Saturday morning after a Friday night with too much to drink (and since the separation, every Friday night seemed to end that way), he had turned up to watch Gary and stood, peeled with cold, feeling as if the wind was playing his bones like a xylophone, and seen children struggle across a pitch churned to a treacle of mud. In five minutes they wore claylike leggings, the ball had become as heavy as a cannonball and the wind purpled their thighs. He remembered one touching moment when a goalkeeper had kicked the ball out and then, as the wind blew it back without anyone else touching it, had to dive dramatically to save his own goal-kick.

'Four-two-four! Four-two-four!' Gary's Company Leader shouted, as if he was communicating.

It was part of the current professional jargon relating to the formation in which a football team should play. Even applied to the professional game, it was, in John's opinion, the imposition of sterile theory upon the most creatively fluid ball-game in the world. Hurled peremptorily at a group of dazed and innocent ten-year-olds, it was as rational as hitting an infant who is dreaming over the head with a copy of *The Interpretation of Dreams*. The words depressed John.

They struck another plangent and familiar chord in his experience of these games. Everything was changing. Week by week, he had been learning the extent of his own failed dreams. Gary had run about so many wintry fields like the vanishing will o' the wisp of John's former expectations, moving remorselessly further and further away from him. He had already virtually lost Carole. She was her mother's daughter, had chosen which side she was on. She would tolerate the times he took them out but, even so young, she had evolved her own discreet code for making their relationship quite formal, like invariably turning her head fractionally when he bent to kiss her, so that her hair on his lips was for him the taste of rejection. Lying in his bed at night, he used to wonder what her mother was telling her about him.

Gary was more supportive. He didn't take sides but when he was with his father he came to him openly, interested in what was happening in his life and concerned to share as much of his own as he could. Yet, in spite of himself, even Gary made John feel excluded – not just because there was so much time when he couldn't be with him but also because, during the times that they were together, it was as if they were speaking in subtly different dialects. Like a parent who has sent his child to elocution lessons, John felt slightly alienated by the gifts he had tried to give Gary.

The football games had come to encapsulate the feeling for John. They were where he had been as a boy and they were a significantly different place. He had acquired his close-dribbling skills and the sudden, killing acceleration in street kickabouts and scratch games under Peeweep Hill where as many as thirty might be playing in one game. He had practised for hours in the house with a ball made of rolled up newspapers tied with string. He had owned his first pair of football boots when he was fifteen.

'Put a pea in yer bloody whistle, ref,' one of the works' team players bellowed.

'Pull your stocking up, Freddie,' the jodhpurs sang.

And John's past and his son's future met in his head and failed to mate. The game wasn't for Gary what it had been for John, a fierce and secret romanticism that fed itself on found scraps – an amazing goal scored and kept pressed in the mind like a perfect rose – a passionate refusal to believe in the boring pragmatism of the conventional authority his teachers represented, a tunnel that ran beneath the crowds of the commonplace and would one day open into a bowl of sunlight and bright grass and the roar of adulation. For Gary it was something you did for the time being, an orderly business of accepted rules and laundered strips and football boots renewed yearly. He could take it or leave it. In a year or two, he would probably leave it. He was starting to play tennis.

John felt in some ways younger than his son. Gary was learning sensible rules of living. Somehow, John never had. The romanticism he had failed to fulfil through football had dogged him all his life. He had tried to smother it in the practicalities of living, had allowed his marriage to close round it like a mausoleum. Katherine, acquisitively middle-class, had overlaid the vagueness of his dreams with the structure of her ambitions. Because of her, they had moved from the flat to the old semi-detached house to the new detached house they couldn't afford, with a mortgage so destructive of every other possibility but the meeting of its terms that sometimes, coming home to his name on the door, he had felt like Dracula pulling the coffin-lid down on himself before a new dawn had a chance to break. Because of Katherine, he had moved out of the factory to be an agent. Though he had come to hate the job, he was still doing it. He hated agreeing with opinions he found un-acceptable. He hated the smiles he clamped on his face going into places. He lived most days between two dreads, the dread of having to fake himself and the dread that it would stop being fakery, that he would get out of bed some morning and there would be no act to put on with his pin-stripe suit. The act would be him.

Finding that Katherine was involved with somebody else had been a kind of bitter relief, since he had been doing the same. The result had been less recrimination than admission of an already accomplished fact. They were finished. They were like two actors who had, unknown to each other, secretly contracted out of a long-running play in which neither believed any more. For both, the new involvements hadn't lasted long.

The affairs had happened not so much for their own sakes as to provide ways of denying their marriage. Once that was denied, John had had to confront the continuing reality of his romanticism. He didn't want a career, he didn't want a big house, he didn't want stability. He wanted a grand passion, he wanted a relationship so real, so intense that it would sustain him till he died.

It was perhaps that rediscovery of himself, the resurgence of vague longings in him that had made him part from Katherine with a grand, flamboyant gesture: He had simply walked out of the house with nothing more than two suit-cases and his collection of jazz records. At thirty-seven he went romantically back out into the world with aspirations as foggy as an adolescent's, some changes of clothes, and records for which he had no record-player. He left the house (in joint names), the car (he had the firm's car), every stick of furniture, the dog, the cat. Only the children he saw as remaining from his unsuccessful pretence of being someone else. And even there the grandeur of his mood had refused to descend to petty specifications. He had made no stipulations about access. Katherine had never tried to stop him seeing them. They were blood of his blood, he always thought. What could a piece of paper and some legal jargon do to alter that?

That day, struggling along the street to where the car was parked away from the house, with his two suitcases and his jazz records in two plastic bags he was praying wouldn't give at the handles, he had felt a great elation. The house lay behind him like a discarded uniform. He wasn't who they had all thought he was. He was a mystery, even to himself. He would be defined by her. Her, wherever she was. Since his teens, lying in bed at night, he had seen her dimly from time to time, as behind a veil, an ectoplasm of limbs, a floating, half-glimpsed smile like a butterfly in moonlight. It was time to take off the veil, to touch the solidity of her presence. He felt as dedicated as a medieval knight. Where would his journey take him?

It took him first of all to 53 Gillisland Road. He rented a single room with a gas-fire that worked on a coin-meter, a papered ceiling which looked as if somebody had started to strip it and then grown bored, a single bed and a moquette suite so larded with the past that John wondered if the settee had doubled as a dinner table. There was a shared kitchen, a shared lavatory. There were in another room two boys from the Western Isles who sang in Gaelic when they were drunk, which appeared to be every night. Their names emerged, from midnight meetings in the kitchen to make coffee, as Calum and Fraser. They were full of oblique jokes only understood by each other, like a touring vaudeville team who hadn't yet adjusted to the local sense of humour. There was Andrew Finlay, a fifty-five-year-old recent div-orcee with a cough that preceded him everywhere like a town-crier. He still couldn't believe what had happened to him. He was given to knocking at doors throughout the evening until he found someone who could confirm for him that he was really there. John became a frequent victim and had learned to dread that cough, like the lead mourner bringing in his wake the funeral for himself that was Andrew Finlay. There were others who remained no more to John than the same song played again and again or a flushing cistern. The house had once been the sort of place Katherine had always wanted and then it had fallen on hard times and been divided into bedsits, so that John felt he had become a lodger in his own past.

It wasn't a happy thought. But he decided that the seediness of his present, ironic in relation to his shimmering mirage of the future, was only temporary. His present was the frog. Come the kiss . . . But he didn't seek it promiscuously. The strength of his romanticism lay in not devaluing the dream. Only once in the three years or more they had been apart had he become seriously involved with a woman, wondered if at last this was the one.

Sally Galbraith worked in one of the offices he visited. She was in her thirties, divorced, with a daughter. She had luxuriant brown hair, gentle eyes and quite marvellous breasts. But it was her smile that had brought her into sharp focus out of the crowd scene that was his thoughts about women. The smile was quite unlike most of the smiles that met him on his rounds – 'do not disturb' signs hung on the mouth while, behind them, the eyes went on with private business. The smile was disturbingly genuine. It was attached to the eyes and seemed personal to him. He felt they were sharing something, an immediate rapport. It was as if he knew her already, but he managed not to say that.

'You're new,' he said instead, and didn't feel it was much more dashingly original.

'Am I? I don't feel as if I am.'

He liked that.

'I would've remembered you.'

'I've just started.'

'Who do I call you?'

'Sally.'

'John.'

He had carried that conversation around with him all day and taken it back at night to his room in Gillisland Road and opened it up and made a meal of it, like a Chinese carry-out. It might have seemed dull on the outside but the secret ingredients were exactly to the taste of his loneliness, all piquant implication and succulent innuendo. Like a gastronome of small talk, he knew exactly what it was made of.

Incredibly enough, he had proved right. On each subsequent visit, the more he assumed the more his assumptions were welcomed. In a month he had asked her out to dinner. He took things slowly. He didn't want the route taken to mar the view he imagined of the arrival. Like someone learning as much as he can about the country to which he wants to emigrate, John studied Sally carefully at meals, on visits to the pictures, in pubs, on walks. He came to know the bleakness of her marriage, interchangeable with a lot of other people's, the fact that she hadn't been with a man in a long time. He met her daughter, Christine, a nine-year-old with a disconcerting habit of talking to her mother as if he wasn't there. He became familiar with the house, a flat with a lot of hanging plants (Sally had done a night class in macramé). Meanwhile, Sally had been taking lessons in John's past.

The night they graduated to bodies seemed to happen by mutual agreement. They had been eating out and were sitting chatting at the end of a good meal when they touched hands and knew at once what both of them wanted for afters. The waiter suggested liqueurs but John settled the bill and they went straight to Sally's flat. The baby-sitter was watching a serial. They had a drink and began to regret their patience in moving towards this moment. John wondered if it was an omnibus edition of the serial. As the baby-sitter was eventually leaving, Christine got out of bed to discuss what she would have to take to school the next day for P.E. There was some doubt, apparently, about whether they would be in the gymnasium or outside.

When Christine went back to her room and while they waited to make sure she was asleep, they kissed and touched each other in delicious preparation. Sally's body was such an exciting place for his hands to wander in and her mouth felt so capable of swallowing his tongue that John was glad of the drinks he had had. He thought they would slow down his reactions nicely. It had been some time now since he had made love and he didn't want to be finished before they had started.

Sally broke away from him and went through to check on Christine. Coming back, she stood in the doorway with her mouth slightly open. She nodded.

'She sleeps through anything,' Sally said. John came across to her and they led each other clumsily through to the bedroom.

The room was a fully furnished annexe of John's dreams. The lighting was from one heavily shaded lamp and it seeped a soft, blueish glow into the room. 'The Blue Grotto', John's mind offered from somewhere, like homage. In the light the yellow walls seemed insubstantial. The bed, with the duvet pulled back, was fawn and inviting.

As they undressed, Sally said, 'I'm sorry about the Wendy House'.

In his feverish preoccupation, John couldn't understand what she meant. He thought at first that it might be a code expression. He wondered bizarrely if she was euphemistically telling him that her period was here. Then he lost his balance slightly taking off a sock and, turning as he steadied himself, he saw the cardboard structure against the wall. Sally was talking about a real Wendy House.

'There's nowhere else to put it,' she said. 'If we put it in Christine's bedroom, it fills the room.'

He didn't mind. It was certainly incongruous here, as if a *femme fatale* were discovered playing with her dolls. But in a way it added to the moment, he convinced himself – like making love in a fairy story. He was naked. Sally was naked. The beauty of her breasts owed nothing to the brassière manufacturers. He approached and touched them, awestruck, as if he had found the holy grail twice. They embraced and fell in luxurious slow motion on to the bed, Sally on top. A part of his mind, like an accountant at an orgy, carefully recorded that she must have had the electric blanket on for some time. It was like making love in hot sand.

Everything went right. In the arrogance of his formidable erection, John knew that he was the scriptwriter for this scene. They passed through their initial clumsiness into a sweet harmony of movements, hands, mouths, legs moving as if they were part of the same being. When he went into her, she smiled with her mouth wide open and said, 'Oh yes, yes, yes'. He was above her now and they were moving towards a meeting he knew he could arrange to the moment.

Then there was a hammering at the outside door, rather as if a yeti were paying a call. With a hand on either side of her head, John paused and looked down at her and shook his head masterfully. He was renewing his purpose when the hammering came again and he heard the letter-box being lifted.

'Sally!'

It sounded as if a Friesian bull had been taking a language course.

'Sally! Ah know ye're in there!'

The expression on Sally's face was like an ice-pack applied to John's scrotum. It was the kind of look the heroine gives in a horror film when she knows the monster has her trapped.

'Oh shite!' Sally said.

'Sally! Open this door! If ye don't want it landin' in the middle of yer loabby.'

'Ignore him,' John suggested unconvincingly.

'I can't, I can't,' Sally said.

John could see her point. It would have been like trying to ignore a hurricane as it blew you away. They had pulled apart from each other now and his penis, treacherous comrade, was already going into hiding. No fun, no me, it seemed to be saying. Suddenly, the atmosphere was that of an air-raid. They stared at each other, paralysed. When they spoke, they found they were whispering.

'Who *is* he?' John mouthed, as if they had time for biographical notes.

'Sally!'

'Alec Manson. He's stone mad.'

The news didn't encourage John in the plan he had been vaguely forming – to pull on his trousers and go to the door. It occurred to him that if Alec Manson happened to be shouting through the letter-box at the time John would probably be blown back along the hall. His nakedness felt *very* naked.

'What does he *do*!' John whispered, not sure himself why he was asking. Was he thinking of pulling rank?

'He's a bouncer in "The Barley Bree Bar".'

John's eyes disappeared briefly under his eyelids. It was roughly equivalent to being told that Alec Manson charged a pack of dingoes protection money. John had only been in 'The Barley Bree' twice in his life and he tended to talk of the occasions the way an explorer might talk about the Amazon Basin. It was regarded as being the roughest pub in Graithnock and that made it very rough. 'If you don't have ten previous convictions, ye're barred,' someone had once told him. But, he told himself, a man's got to offer to do what a man's terrified to do.

'You want me to see about this?' he quavered quietly.

'Ah can see a light in there!' the voice was announcing to the immediate neighbourhood. 'There's somebody in there.'

'Oh my God, no!'

The panic the thought had engendered in Sally would have been unflattering in another situation. Here, with the guardian of 'The Barley Bree' sending his voice along the hall like a flame-thrower, it seemed no more than a perfectly reasonable response, confirmation of the obvious.

'Right! We can do it the easy way or the hard way! With a handle or without a handle! Ah'm countin tae ten! One!'

It wasn't the kind of accomplishment you would have expected a voice like that to have but they couldn't just wait there and see if he got stuck at seven. They scrabbled from the bed, moving in quite a few directions at once. The room became a flurry of movement without progress, as if they were caught in a film being run backwards and forwards at the wrong speed.

Sally ran naked to the bedroom door and then ran back. John bent down and put on a sock.

'Two!'

Sally plumped one pillow, dented the other. Some desperate plan seemed to be forming in her mind.

'Three!'

As John bent down to pick up his clothes, Sally shoved

them under the bed with her foot on her way to pick up the Laura Ashley nightdress that was draped across a wickerwork chair.

'Four!'

'Hey!' John hissed. Sally's head, emerging from the neck of the nightdress was shaking vigorously as she stared, wild-eyed, at John. 'No time!' she screamed silently.

'Five!'

Sally smoothed down her nightdress, made a couple of meaningless passes at the duvet. She turned to see John whirling in the middle of the floor, as if he had chosen this moment to practise miming a dervish.

'Six!'

Sally pointed at the Wendy House, pushed John towards it. He looked at her. She opened the cardboard door and jabbed her finger ferociously at the interior several times. He couldn't believe it.

'Seven!'

He believed it. He crouched inside while Sally closed the door on him. He heard her sprint across the bedroom and then, at the door, begin to walk along the hall.

'Alec?'

Her voice sounded so sleepy. The other voice had started to say 'eight' and trailed off. To John, huddled in his Wendy House, the blue tinge of the light had taken on a sinister quality, moonscape, jowls of the dead.

'Alec? Is that you, Alec?'

John could hear the yawn in her voice from where he was. Listening to that expertly feigned sleepiness induced in him an agony of ambivalence. (The door was being opened. Godzilla comes.) He couldn't believe that his Sally of the gentle eyes and honest smile could be such an actress. There were questions he had to think over, though not now. The other part of the feeling was the fervent hope that she really was as good an actress as she sounded. A lot depended on her performance.

'It took you long enough.'

'I was sleeping, Alec. Here, let me help you.'

Alec's feet were thudding all over the hall and there were noises that might have been several bodies hitting off the walls. He sounded like a drunken regiment. An alarming proximity of heavy breathing made John think they had reached the bedroom door. It might have been John's imagination but he had a suspicion of the presence of foetid breath, as of a carnivore exhaling close at hand.

'You've had somebody in here!'

John was suddenly aware of the fragility of Wendy Houses. A tunnel would have been handy.

'That's right. Four men.'

John didn't see the joke. Pacify, pacify, he was thinking.

'You've had somebody in here!'

'I was sleeping!'

'Maybe. Ah'm goin' to check.'

There was an amazing amount of noise, which was apparently Alec going through to the living-room. Whatever previous convictions had qualified Alec for admission to 'The Barley Bree', burglary wasn't one of them. He made a small riot of coming back towards the bedroom. Sally was still insisting on helping him. John wondered how you did that. It must have been like guiding a stampede.

'That's you now,' she was saying. 'There we are. Satisfied now?'

'Okay, love. Ah know ye're tellin' the truth When Ah saw that the telly was off.'

John was relieved that Alec's deductive powers weren't in proportion to his imagined bulk. John was holding himself well back from the cut-out windows of the Wendy House. Christine or Sally had stuck cellophane across them and John decided now that the light was like trying to see underwater – the mysteries of the deep. He was aware of Sally's white nightdress with red flowers eddying uncertainly around the room. A huge dark shape swayed beside her.

'Ah haven't seen you for a fortnight,' Alec growled gently.

'You're seeing me now. Come on, lie down. You look whacked.'

'A fortnight,' Alec said.

'You need some rest.'

'Ā fortnight.'

Once Alec got hold of an idea, he didn't give it up easily. He wasn't moving. The thought that he hadn't seen Sally for a fortnight appeared to have transfixed him, like some great revelation not vouchsafed to many.

'A fortnight.'

'A fortnight, Alec.'

Something was biting into John's unstockinged foot savagely. The pain was becoming unbearable but he was afraid to move. He was also terrified that if he changed the position of his other leg the knee would crack. He could be the first recorded case of a stiff knee proving fatal. Alec spoke an eerie echo of John's thought.

'It's a good thing for whoever it is that he isny here.'

The logic was opaque but John understood it perfectly.

'That's right,' Sally said.

'A fortnight,' Alec said.

In a moment of wild panic, John could imagine the cryptic exchange going on until his emaciated body was lifted too late, from the Wendy House. There was a noise that he was sure meant Alec had sat down on the bed. He hoped that was a good sign. Something hit the Wendy House and it buckled slightly and rattled against his head. He almost called out in panic.

'Oops,' Alec said.

'Watch Christine's Wendy House.'

No, no, you bloody mug, John was screaming to himself. Don't draw his attention to it. What Wendy House? There *is* no Wendy House. He might come over and inspect it for damage.

' 'S all right, love,' Alec said. 'Just ma shoe.'

The other shoe hit the floor.

'Lie down, Alec.'

'Hm?'

'Let me get your jacket off. That's it. Right, lie down.'

'Uh-huh.'

The bed squeaked on its castors. Alec sighed, a sound like a small whirlwind. There was silence. John strained into it desperately. He was about to move his leg when he froze the movement, biting his lip.

'Sally,' Alec said.

Sally said nothing. A couple of minutes passed. Someone was at the door of the Wendy House. Although John had seen Sally's nightdress move towards him, he was still tensed as the door opened, as though it might have been Alec in drag. Sally was crouched looking in at him, her forefinger to her lips. Did she think he might be singing? She held his clothes with one arm against her body. With the other she motioned him to follow.

Tiptoeing after her, John couldn't escape the hallucinatory feeling that he was in a fairy story after all. And John tiptoed from his little house past the sleeping giant and followed the good fairy. He glanced very quickly at Alec in case looking at him might waken him. He seemed gross in sleep. His mouth, like every other part of him, appeared to make more noise than was consistent with performing its basic function. His lips flapped in the wind of his breathing.

In the hall, John studied his heel briefly and saw the imprint of the face of the miniature doll – savage little household god. As he dressed very swiftly, Sally stroked his hair a couple of times. She mouthed his ear. Was she mad? He had noticed that before about women, how quickly they forgot risk when they were feeling roused. At the open door she held his arm.

'It's all right now,' she whispered. 'It's just that he's impossible when he's drunk.'

John nodded.

'In the morning I'll send him packing. No problem. He'll go like a lamb.'

John nodded.

'I don't see him now, you know. That's all finished. There's nothing between us. It's just taking him time to get over it. He's living in the past. But he has no rights here. And he knows it.'

John nodded. Of course. That's why he was taking up two-thirds of her bed.

'Listen. I hope this hasn't put you off.'

John nodded and then changed to shaking his head. Not at all. Why should the possibility of being beaten to death every time you got into bed put you off?

'Sally!'

She winked, kissed the tips of her fingers and touched them to his lips.

'It's all right, Alec,' John heard her call as he came downstairs, letting the darkness take him into it. She rattled the milk bottles she had put out when the baby-sitter left. 'I'm just locking up.'

John had brooded on the significance of that evening ever since. Sometimes, without warning, fragments of it would occur to him. He would hear 'Sally! Sally!' or see her face, distorted with panic, as she lay beneath him. Such moments came to him isolated and complete, inexplicable but stubbornly there, ciphers the pilgrim found along his way. But in what direction were they pointing him? Their repetitiousness suggested he hadn't resolved them. They were liable to turn up anywhere, in a pub, in the car, at a football match on a wet evening.

'Tackle, Freddie, tackle!' Jodhpurs was calling.

Gary had the ball. As Freddie lunged towards him, Gary drew the ball back and then threaded it neatly through

Freddie's legs and ran round him, leaving him stranded.
'Nutmegged him,' John muttered to himself. It was a way
in which professional players hated to be beaten, perhaps
because it made you look so silly – your legs, the very basis
of your craft, being reduced to the role of a triumphal arch
for the parade of your opponent's skills. John was absurdly
pleased. He glanced along at Jodhpurs as if he had taken
revenge on her loud ignorance.

'Sally! Sally!'

He had seen her since then in her office and once had a
drink with her (not in 'The Barley Bree'). She gave him
occasional reports on the nocturnal activities of Alec
Manson. His visits were apparently becoming less frequent.
'He's coming to his senses,' Sally had said but John wasn't
convinced that would ever be a permanent place of residence
for Alec. Sally seemed still to expect that they would some
time continue where they had left off, once Alec's supposed
refusal to forget the past had died of exhaustion. John wasn't
so sure.

He had thought about it a lot and and he believed (how
could he be sure?) that his uncertainties didn't come from
fear of Alec. Now that he understood the risks, the location
and habits of the dragon as it were, he felt he could work
out ways to reach the maiden safely. But he suspected she
was no longer the maiden he had thought she was. He still
relished the memory of her body and would have liked to
go back there but – such was the fervour of his dreams – he
could only do it with his faith intact. Paradoxically, to
accept her offer of herself would have been for him to
diminish her unless he did it on terms of belief in her.

That belief had been undermined to some extent. 'A
fortnight' had been carved on John's mind. Alec had said
it as if it meant a long time in his terms. Surely he wasn't
always drunk and surely he didn't always go there just to
sleep. John thought perhaps Sally had been lying to him.
And, besides that central matter, his sense of Sally had been

irredeemably altered. 'Oh shite!' was something he would never have imagined her saying, a glimpse of another person, just as the nature of Alec had been. How had she become involved with a bouncer from 'The Barley Bree'?'

One of the times John had been in that pub, a group of women in their thirties had been skipping rope, one at each end spinning the rope and the others jumping in turn, repeating the rhymes of their childhood. It had been an arresting scene to witness coming in off the street, rather like pushing open a door in an industrial West of Scotland town and entering the atmosphere of a frontier saloon in the American West. It was all loud laughter and the abandonment of bouncing breasts and shouted encouragement. A bystander, who appeared to be a regular, explained to John how the scene had come about, as if it were the most natural thing in the world.

It seemed one of the women had been shopping before coming into the pub and happened to mention over her drink that she had been buying a new clothes-rope. There had been talk of how times had changed for all of them, how rope had at one time meant not the boring duty of hanging out washing but the carefree pleasure of jumping rope. Someone had said it would have been great to go back there so they had gone, there and then, challenging one another to demonstrate their skills. The man who was telling John of the background to the event seemed to be concerned to make it clear that this didn't happen every day in the pub. That didn't make the place much less remarkable in John's eyes. 'The Barley Bree' might not be the kind of pub where big, buxom women skipped rope every day like maenads but it was the kind of pub where, if they had the notion to do so and a rope was handy, they just carried on – and the barman looked on with a kind of reluctant indulgence, perhaps because there were other uses to which a rope could be put.

An acquaintance of John claimed to have been in 'The

Barley Bree' one Saturday afternoon when a dog and bitch decided to consummate their passion in a corner. Nobody had paid particular attention, John's acquaintance said, and when he had expressed his amazement to someone sitting near him, the man had answered, 'What can ye expect? They see it every day in the hoose.'

The story could have been apocryphal but it matched John's sense of the place. Sally's association with 'The Barley Bree' changed John's sense of her. The enchanted bedroom was surrounded by quicksand. He wasn't judging her life or anybody else's. It wasn't in his nature to do that. He was simply looking for a habitation for his private longings, a place where he could share them with someone. Sally had not only made him think that it might be impossible to share them with her, she had also made him wonder if it would ever be possible to share them with anyone.

He would sit in his room, reading the greasy moquette pattern of his suite into a significance as mysterious as the Rosetta stone and, whatever it meant, the message was a sad one. The incomprehensible Gaelic songs would drift hauntingly around him like the sound of all the lost dreams of which his was just another. The cistern would gurgle from time to time. Andrew Finlay would cough nervously through the evening, as if embarrassedly trying to attract the world's attention. John would look through the jazz records for which he had no record-player ('Out of the Galleon' was the one he held the most) and they became in his melancholy a symbol of his life, the mute longing, the music that couldn't be heard.

The ridiculous image of himself hiding in the Wendy House began to seem more than an accidental moment in his life. There were perhaps times, it appeared to him, when a fleeting gesture or a spontaneous stance could freeze into definition, like a head stamped on a coin, and become your essential currency. For a great footballer it might be one game or one goal. For another man, the moment of his marriage. John dreaded that for him it might be his sojourn in the Wendy House. That might become the prison of his own sense of himself. Perhaps that's who he was – a ridiculous naked man with one sock on hiding in a cardboard house, waiting for his own true love.

'Ah can't wait to get home an' get the wife's knickers off,' one of the players in the works' game said to another. 'They're killin' me.'

'Aye,' the other one answered. 'If they had pints laid out across the park, Ah would cover the ground a lot quicker.'

'Referee!' somebody shouted. 'There's a man here wankin'. Is that a foul?'

The player who had been adjusting his shorts responded at once: 'Only when the balls are in play.'

The harsh self-confidence of everything they said and did was like a mockery of John's uncertainty about himself. He stood on the path of neutral ground between the two games and felt his position as an irrelevant spectator to be a just expression of himself. In his attempts to adjust to the kind of life Katherine had wanted, he had lost the rough spontaneity he had come from, the ability the works' game was celebrating to take whatever life offered and shrug and have another pint in a way that suggested you hadn't expected much more of the devious bastard. Yet, leaving that behind, he hadn't managed to reach the place that presumably Gary and most of these other boys were practising to get to, where you knew all the practical social rules and could apply them to your advantage. He felt as if he didn't fit anywhere, didn't seem to know what position he was supposed to be playing, might never know what the score was when the final whistle blew.

When it blew for the end of Gary's game, he was glad. Gary's team had won three–two.

'Shake hands! Shake hands!' Gary's Company Leader shouted unnecessarily.

All the boys were shaking hands anyway. John approved

in theory of the idea that they should. But the formality
with which they did it seemed to him false, an adult
imposition on their natural reactions, like a bow-tie on a
tee-shirt. As they came off the field, some parents joined
them on the walk back to the clubhouse.

'Well played, Freddie. Well played!'

John settled for gently slapping the back of Gary's head
as he passed and Gary's right hand hinted at a wave of
acknowledgement. It was their relationship in miniature:
affection inhibited by circumstances. As John waited for
Gary to come back out, he wondered if Katherine had told
the children that the divorce had been finalised. He thought
that she must have told them. But in the car he glanced at
Gary and wondered.

'What did you think, Dad?' Gary asked.

'You played well, son.'

'Made a mess of that corner.'

'The wind was deceptive. What did Helenio Herrera say?'

The name of the famous football manager was their
private joke about the Company Leader.

'He's daft. Know what he said? "You didn't die for the
jerseys." You'd think it was the World Cup.'

John agreed with Gary but the distance in years between
them made that agreement strange. At Gary's age, John
would have taken the Company Leader seriously. He would
have wanted to die for the jerseys. Gary's perspective on
things disconcerted him, as it often did.

'Gary. Your mother's told you about the divorce?'

'Uh-huh.'

Gary had been fiddling with the glove compartment. He
took out a sheet of petrol stamps and studied them like a
philatelist.

'How do you feel about that?'

'Doesn't make any difference to us, does it?'

'No, that's right.'

'Well.'

'Any word of the other house yet?'

'Not yet. Mum says there's plenty of time. We don't have to move out of this one for a while.'

Gary seemed calm. John didn't want to disturb that calmness. He didn't say anything else till they pulled up at the door.

'Thanks, Dad. So when will I see you? We've got a game on Saturday.'

'I'll be there. With my rattle.'

Gary was surprised when John got out of the car as well.

'There's something I've to collect,' John said.

They came up the path together. The door opened before they reached it and Katherine was there, forestalling the need for John to come into the house. She was already holding out the envelope.

'Well, Dad.' Gary was standing awkwardly between them. 'Thanks. See you on Saturday?'

'Sure. You go and have your bath.'

Katherine was gazing out into the street, waiting for them to finish. She was wearing a black leather jump-suit, unzipped to show her cleavage, and high heels that almost qualified as stilts. John had noticed that any time they met each other by appointment, she had a new outfit on and was carefully coiffed. She seemed to like to show him what he had lost. When Gary went into the house, she smiled pityingly and handed John the sealed envelope as if it contained his extradition papers from Eden. The envelope felt very light.

'Fourteen years don't weigh much,' John said.

'Did they ever?'

John wasn't sure he knew what that was supposed to mean, but that wasn't a feeling alien to him when talking to Katherine. He recognised a technique with which he was familiar. Katherine always preferred gestures to actions. Her conversation had always been rich in glib phrases and rhetorical questions that, on examination, frequently defied any search for substance. But they sounded good at the time.

'It's all here?' John asked.

'A cheque for four thousand pounds. And goodbye.'

John nodded and turned away and then turned back.

'Oh, Katherine. I'm not sure this is adequate compensation. I may appeal to an industrial tribunal.'

She closed the door. In the car he had to open the envelope, just to make sure it didn't contain a joke card. There it was: a cheque for four thousand pounds, signed 'Katherine Hannah'. It was his agreed share from the sale of the house, once the mortgage was settled. It was less than Katherine was getting, because he didn't want to cause the children any financial problems besides the others they must be having. And Katherine had everything else, the furniture, the car.

The signature offended him. It was the punch line to the joke he felt his life had become. His life had been used by her and now she was paying him off, like a hired hand whose services were no longer required. This was his redundancy money. He put the cheque back in its envelope, put the envelope in his inside pocket and drove to Gillisland Road.

He thought of the maintenance he had been paying since they separated, more than he could afford, and he seemed to feel the money dwindle in his pocket. There was no point in using it as a down-payment on a small house because he wouldn't be able to keep up the mortgage. Knowing the cheque was due tonight, he had been vaguely looking towards it as a partial solution to his problems. Now that he had it, he dreaded it would be lost like loose change down the widening cracks in the financial basis of his life and he would be left with nothing to show for it. The cheque served only to highlight the hopelessness he saw ahead, years of scrabbling to meet his financial commitments, of travelling between Gillisland Road and wherever Katherine bought a house or wherever Gary was playing football or

Carole was singing in a concert with her choir. He saw himself driving through the time ahead like a demented delivery man, leaving his affection where other people could collect it. When he parked the car in Gillisland Road, he couldn't bring himself to go up into his room, as if he would be volunteering to accept his fate.

He left the car and decided to go for a drink. Walking, he was glad he had made the remark about the industrial tribunal. His mind clung to the joke like a lifebelt keeping him afloat a little longer.

4

Death of a spinster

Each weekday was mapped. When the digital alarm went, she would press the snooze mechanism two separate times so that she would have about ten minutes more in bed. When she got out of bed, she would reset the alarm for next day, making sure each time that it was set for a.m. Tomorrow was promised.

The day took her to itself like an assembly line. Routine precludes the time to weep. She showered, wearing the floral shower-cap. (She only washed her hair at weekends.) Soaping her body was a sensual ceremony and she always noted how firm she still was in her late fifties, taking a dispassionate inventory of herself like someone viewing an empty house. She dried and dressed in the clothes she had laid out the previous evening.

She clicked on the already filled kettle. She turned on the gas till it clicked alight and put on it the two eggs waiting in their panful of water. She gave the eggs three minutes from the time the water boiled. She toasted one slice of bread and buttered it. She poured the hot water into the cup containing instant coffee and one sweetener. She put one egg, taken out of the pan with a tablespoon and dried with a teacloth, into an eggcup and the other in the saucer beside it. She breakfasted.

The dishes were gathered and put in the basin with the remainder of the hot water from the kettle which was then refilled. She always noted how scuffed cheap plastic gets with use. The make-up she applied was a suggestion of who she might be. The timed walk to wait for the bus that was invariably busy brought the brief satisfaction of seeing the tired man with the gentle eyes. He seemed unhappy in a way that made her want to talk to him but she never had.

The working day was full of apparent differences that turned out to be the same. She typed letters and dispensed stationery and dealt with problems that didn't really matter. At lunchtime she had a snack alone in the town and looked at some shops and made sure she was back in time to talk for about twenty minutes with Marion Bland. The afternoon was the same as the morning.

No matter what shopping she had to do, she was home in time to watch the news on television. The strangeness of the world appalled her but she couldn't resist watching the strangeness. She ate at seven. Lasagne was her favourite. The evening was usually television programmes she had ringed in *Radio Times* and *TV Times*. At nine she had her sherry. Sometimes she had one sherry, sometimes two. Three was an orgy.

The evening was also the most dangerous part of her life. Time was less obedient then. Sometimes Margaret and John Hislop came. She didn't always enjoy their visits. They often seemed to be using her as an audience, allowing her to look on at their cosy warmth and predictable banter. But they were the nearest thing to family she had. Sometimes she thought over things that Marion had said and wondered what Marion's life was like. Sometimes she talked aloud to the photograph of her nephew, Ronnie Milligan, who was in Canada. Sometimes the fantasies came almost more fierce than she could bear and containing images she could hardly admit. On such nights she took two Mogadon instead of one.

These trivia she strung like charms about the pulse of her life. One day the charms broke. An unscheduled car drove straight in between shopping and talking to Marion. The crowd didn't know her. One man leaning close to her lips heard them give up the meaning of who she had been. In that whisper of breath, that indistinct sound, her life was caught in a moment – politely unheard.

Her lightness was loaded into an ambulance. How slim she had stayed. Behind her she was leaving an unpaid gas bill and Marion bereft of about twenty minutes of daily conversation. Her nephew would hear of it later. Margaret and John Hislop would feel bad about having found her so dull. A handsome restaurant waiter she used to give lavish tips would wonder intermittently what had happened to her and his thoughts would be a kind of requiem, duly paid for. The dishes were unwashed. The alarm would be unanswered.

Stripping off her prim clothes, they were amazed at the vision they saw. Her body was sensuous in rich underwear. The brassiere and the pants were of pale green, sheer silk, beneath which the dark pubic hair shimmered like Atlantis. They went on with what they had to do, unaware that they had witnessed the stubborn resplendence of unfulfilled dreams.

5

The prisoner

'All right, Rafferty,' the governor said. 'Good luck. And let's hope we won't be seeing you again.'

The next one he certainly would be seeing again.

McQueen: over the past twenty years more time in prison than out of it. Recidivist. Always the same crime: burglary without violence but also burglary without the slightest indication of ever stopping. Show McQueen a big house and he wanted to screw it. The Don Juan of burglary. His only saving grace as a burglar was his inefficiency. But at least inside he had tended to behave. And now this.

The governor closed the file. He prepared himself for McQueen's presence, the rumpled hair, the heavy shoulders, the puzzlingly introverted eyes. The feeling that you might never get through to him. Conversations with a totem pole.

Without looking up, the governor knew that the assistant governor was watching him. He also knew, irritatedly, the way he was watching him: that look of those who wait for someone else to see the light. The governor hated that look, smugness like bell metal. The assistant governor was like a Jehovah's Witness of the hard line, always ready to canvass for his cause, always patient before the benightedness of others, always convinced that phoney liberals would eventually see the error of their ways.

The governor looked up and saw the expression that was

pointed towards him like a Bible tract. Let us be righteous and burn the other bastards in hellfire.

'Okay,' the governor said. 'Let's have him in.'

'This is a bad one, chief.'

The governor wondered where the assistant governor got his dialogue.

'Uh-huh,' he said. 'Let's have him in.'

'You want me in with you on this one?'

'No, Frank.'

'After what he's done?'

'I know McQueen.'

'We all thought we knew McQueen.'

'Frank. If I shout for help, you come in with the machine-gun.'

Levity was the best defence against the assistant governor. Humour was a foreign language to him. If you wanted him to laugh, you had to tell him it was a joke. He had his customary reaction of mild affront and went out and officiously ushered in McQueen, giving the governor a last significant look: help is at hand.

McQueen came in pleasantly and stood in front of the governor's desk. The governor decided not to tell him to sit down. This was a stand-up problem. McQueen returned the governor's look and almost smiled and gazed out of the window. The governor tried not to like that crumpled face that looked as if it might have come out of the womb asking for directions and still not received an answer.

'McQueen.'

'Sur!'

The governor felt that McQueen's respect was subtly disrespectful. He invariably addressed the governor as 'Sir' but he invariably used the inflection of his West of Scotland dialect, as if reminding him that they didn't quite speak the same language. 'Sur' was the fifth-column in the standard English McQueen affected when speaking to the governor.

'You know what this is about.'

'Yes, sur.'

'Why?'

McQueen shrugged.

'Sur?'

'McQueen. You were obviously unhappy throughout the Christmas meal. Officer Roberts warned you three times. Christmas is a bad time for the men. The slightest bit of trouble could cause a riot. And what did you do? At the end of the meal you smashed your plate on the floor. You jumped on to the table and danced through all the other empty plates. You broke three chairs. And it took four warders to get you out of there. Is that a fair report?'

'Two chairs, sur. One of them wouldny brek.'

The governor decided to let the pedantry pass.

'Just tell me why, McQueen.'

He looked off into the distance that lay outside the window and the governor was aware again of the opaque quality of McQueen's eyes. They were the eyes – the governor had to admit it – of a visionary. A private, bizarre, non-conformist visionary. You could never be sure what was going on in McQueen's head but you could always be sure it was something. If only he would keep it in there, whatever it was, the governor thought. McQueen looked back at the governor and the governor briefly felt their roles reversed. He knew that McQueen was going to tell him, but with something that felt like condescension. It was as if McQueen had set the governor a simple problem and he was saddened that the governor couldn't solve it. He would tell him but in the manner of a disappointed teacher reluctantly admitting that his pupil hadn't made much progress.

'The turkey, sur,' he said.

'The turkey?'

'The turkey, sur.'

'What was wrong with the turkey?'

'Did you see the turkey, sur?'

'I saw the turkey. McQueen. I *ate* the turkey. McQueen.

It may interest you to know that during any working day I eat the same food as the inmates. I don't have lunches sent up from the Ritz. I *care* about this establishment. I think every inmate in here deserves to be punished. But punished in specific ways. And spoiling the food isn't one of them. I check the kitchen every single day. That was a very special Christmas meal we made. The turkey was of high quality. I *tasted* it!'

'It wasn't the taste.'

'I beg your pardon?'

'Sur. It wasn't the taste. Sur.'

'No, no. That's not what I mean. You thought the turkey tasted all right?'

'I've tasted better, sur. But it was all right.'

The governor looked down at the impeccable order of his desk. There was the matching set of marled fountain-pen and propelling pencil which his wife had given him years ago on his first senior appointment. There was the photograph of Catriona and Kim and Jason, looking laundered. There were the books of reference, sandbags between him and procedural error. There was the correspondence waiting to be signed, not an edge of a sheet out of place. The only thing that hinted at the invading chaos of a life like McQueen's was the big desk blotter. It was covered in hieroglyphics, countless comments and signatures that had come out backwards, overlaying one another and creating a complex palimpsest as difficult to decipher as an ancient manuscript. He would have to renew it soon.

Looking at the blotter, he felt the familiar feeling that came from talking to McQueen. He was trying to define the feeling. About three years ago, Catriona and he had gone to a play. It was the last time they had been to the theatre. They had sat through an hour-and-three-quarters during which people did things that had no connection with anything they had done before and made remarks to one another that seemed to come out of thin air. One character spoke for ten minutes at one point without interruption and then the play went on as if she hadn't opened her mouth. As far as Catriona and he were concerned, she might as well not have. They stayed for the whole performance out of a kind of baffled guilt, exchanging looks. Were they the only ones who hadn't read the guide-book? At the interval, an ageing man who had two attractive girls with him had said, 'Surrealist,' into a gin and tonic. Perhaps McQueen was a surrealist.

'So the turkey tasted all right,' the governor said. 'So what was the problem? The presentation? Did the waiter serve you from the wrong side?'

Something resembling relaxed enjoyment surfaced in McQueen's eyes and sank again, like a fish in a polluted pool. McQueen had liked the remark. The governor had a moving glimpse of what it might have been like to talk to McQueen outside the walls.

'Well?'

'You ate it, sur?'

'I've told you that.'

'Ye didn't notice anything, sur?'

'I noticed it tasted very good. And so did the roast potatoes. And the other vegetable. What was it again? And the stuffing. And the cranberry sauce. We even gave you cranberry sauce!'

'And that's all, sur?'

'What more did you want?'

'Naw, sur. I meant that's all you noticed? The taste, like.'

'What else is there, man?'

McQueen looked at the governor as if he had only just realised what a wag he was. He shook his head: I may look simple but you don't catch me out as easily as that.

'McQueen! For heaven's sake! If you don't tell me *now* what was wrong with the turkey . . .'

McQueen pursed his lips. His expression suggested he was being asked to tell a watch the time.

'It was round,' he said.

The governor stared at him. He was back watching that incomprehensible play.

'It was round?' he asked with the involuntary tone of someone being admitted to a deep secret.

'The turkey was round, sur,' McQueen confirmed.

The governor recovered quickly.

'Of course, the turkey was round. I saw the bloody thing. The turkey was bloody round.' The governor paused. He had used a swear-word. The governor never swore in front of the men. He looked sternly at McQueen as though trying to convince McQueen that he was the one who had sworn. 'So what?'

'Turkeys aren't round, sur.'

'I know turkeys aren't round, McQueen. You don't have to tell me that. That was *part* of a turkey. What you ate was *part* of a turkey.'

'Which part was that, sur?'

'What do you mean?'

'What part of a turkey's round?'

'There's no part of a turkey that's round.' The governor hesitated. 'Or if there is, I wouldn't know. That's not the point. You ate turkey. You had turkey for your Christmas dinner. I'm telling you that. You ate turkey, McQueen.'

McQueen looked at the floor stubbornly, unconvinced. A small dawn rose in the governor's eyes. McQueen had been in for six years this time. Before that, he had been outside only for brief spells over a period of twelve years. Other inmates referred to McQueen's time outside as taking his holidays. McQueen was simply out of touch with the ways of the world.

'McQueen,' the governor said. 'It was turkey roll.'

'What, sur?'

'What you ate. It was turkey roll.'

McQueen considered the possibility.

'It's a process, McQueen. A modern process. You take a

lot of turkeys and make them into a turkey roll. With machinery. You *refine* the turkeys.'

'How do ye do that, sur?'

The governor looked away.

'You. Pass them through machinery.'

'What? Everything, sur?'

'How would I know, McQueen? I suppose you take the feathers off. Just accept the fact, man. Everybody else does. It was turkey roll.'

'It wasn't turkey, sur.'

'McQueen. Turkey roll *is* turkey. Everybody accepts that. It's what a lot of people eat.'

'Then they're not eatin' turkey, sur. Turkey roll, as ye call it, isn't turkey. It may be *like* turkey. But it's not turkey.'

'It is turkey! What else would it be?'

McQueen was taking the question seriously.

'See when they refine it, sur? What is the exact process?'

The governor was watching McQueen, realising something. But McQueen was too caught up in pursuit of his own ideas to notice. The governor observed him from a distance, like a business-manager full of grave responsibilities looking out of his office window to see a grown-up layabout, who should know better, chasing after butterflies in the park.

'See what I mean, sur? What happens when they turn a turkey into turkey roll? What is it they do, sur? Do you know? Do I know? Do any of the ordinary people know? They take out the bones. Right? They must take out the bones, sur. But nowadays, who knows? Maybe they powder them, sur. And mix it in with the whole mish-mash. But what *exactly* do they do? What is the machinery *like*, sur? And.' McQueen paused with the look of a man who has found the incontrovertible point, the argument with which you must agree. 'What else do they *put in*? It's guaranteed they put in something, sur. If turkey roll's not a substitute for turkey, why not just have the turkey? Eh?' McQueen was smiling in triumph. 'It's cheaper. And what are they doing to make it cheaper? They could put any kind of crap in there, sur, and we wouldn't know. Preservatives. Bits of dead dogs for all we know. We're being had, sur. Everybody's being had. Turkey roll isn't turkey. Sur.'

The governor was looking at McQueen. What he had realised was that McQueen was enjoying this. All the men did that. Let out of their routine for any purpose, they contrived to make an event of it. It was part of the emotional economy of prison, like a man going to be hanged who decides he'll try to enjoy the walk to the gallows. The governor understood that.

But McQueen's was an extreme case. He had just been brought up from solitary on a very grave breach of discipline. It could be incitement to riot. And he had contrived to turn his appearance before the governor into a metaphysical discussion on what constitutes a turkey. Was he serious?

The governor studied McQueen, who let himself be studied without apparent discomfort. The intensity of McQueen's commitment to the great turkey question seemed unreal but his reaction to the Christmas dinner had been real enough. You had to wonder if round turkeys were just an excuse but when you looked at McQueen they sure enough felt like a reason.

Prison magnified trivia. Everything came at you as if it was under a microscope. If a man you didn't like raised his forefinger, it looked like an obelisk. The governor had known a man who was killed for not paying the tobacco he owed. The tobacco, carefully used, would have made five cigarettes. The governor had a blessedly brief vision of the terrible complexities with which he was dealing. Habit came to his rescue.

'McQueen,' the governor said. 'That's it? Because the turkey was round?'

'It wasn't turkey, sur.'

'It was turkey roll.'

'We were promised turkey.'

'Everybody else seemed satisfied.'

'That's up to them.'

The governor contemplated the strange wildness of McQueen's behaviour and gave it up.

'You're back to solitary, McQueen,' he said. 'Till I decide. I see no justification for your behaviour. I don't even see that you're sorry for it. Are you? I mean, was that the only way you could express yourself?'

McQueen shrugged.

'You said it yerself, sur. Ye can't complain to the waiter, can ye?'

The governor wondered how he was supposed to have said it himself. Then he remembered having mentioned the idea of a waiter serving from the wrong side. There it was again, tangential attempts to meet. One of us, the governor thought, is wrong. Or perhaps we both are. He hadn't time to pursue the thought.

'McQueen. I'm disappointed in you. You know the score here. Every man in here is a long-termer from another place. This is where you get a chance to prepare for outside. You know this is an easy ticket. We're trying to make a transition here. From hard jails to the real world.'

'That's the real world, sur? Broken promises? Synthetic turkey?'

'The interview's over, McQueen. Don't you understand that? And you didn't get the job. I've tried to give you a chance. We'll do it my way now. And you'll just listen. In the meantime you're back yourself. I don't want any rotten apples in my barrel. You're a mug. You've maybe just worked your ticket to a real jail. I'll let you know. In the meantime, stew in your juice. I hope you enjoy it. Thing is, you're not even a violent man. Then you do this. Hoof it.'

As McQueen turned, one thing was still niggling at the governor's mind.

'McQueen!'

McQueen stopped, turned round.

'You ate the turkey.'

'Sorry, sur?'

'You ate the turkey. And then you ate the pudding. Was the pudding all right, by the way? Was that to your taste?'

'It wasn't really, sur.'

'Oh. What was wrong with that?'

'Ah don't like a cold thing and a warm thing put together.'

'You mean the ice-cream and the hot apple tart?'

'That's right, sur.'

'I hope you like the menu better where you're going.'

McQueen was turning away again.

'But you miss the point,' the governor said.

McQueen turned back, practised in patience.

'You *ate* the turkey,' the governor said. 'You *ate* the pudding. You ate everything. And then you made your protest. Why?'

McQueen gave him that habitual look that suggested the world was out to con him.

'Ah was hungry, sur,' he said.

The governor was left staring into the remark. It opened like a window on to a place he had never been. He saw McQueen sitting eating his meal in the big hall. Around him were faces that wouldn't have been out of place on Notre Dame Cathedral. McQueen was grumbling but nobody else was giving him any support. McQueen was hungry, so he ate everything and then exploded. The precision was where the governor had never been, the precision of passion, the risk of choosing the moment when you try to express utterly what you feel. McQueen, the governor understood with a dismay that would quickly bury the understanding in disbelief like dead leaves, was capable of something of which the governor was not. McQueen was capable of freedom.

The assistant governor opened the door and looked in.

'Well?' he said.

'We'll see. He goes back down today. Then I'll decide.'

'It's a bad one. We don't need that stuff here.'

'I know that. We'll see.'

The assistant governor contrived to make a nod look negative and went out.

The governor started to sign his mail. When he was finished, he would inspect the kitchens. Then he would have lunch with the assistant governor and Mrs Caldwell, the teacher. They would discuss which inmates might be capable of sitting an external examination, the advisability of an evening creative writing class under a visiting teacher and the case of Branson, who believed he was a genius not being published simply because he was in prison. The afternoon was exactly scheduled. He would leave a little early this evening because he was speaking to the Rotary Club in the nearest town, where he lived. Catriona and the children would be asleep by the time he got back. It was an early rise tomorrow. It was his day off and it was their day for visiting his parents. The drive was long and boring and it only gave them three hours at his parents' house. But maybe that was just as well. His mother was a woman who had turned into a compendium of elusive ailments which she recited as if they were conversation. His father would sit apparently stunned into silent awe at the agonies she went through. They would all get back just in time for bed. As he worked, the governor was vaguely aware of an image prowling the perimeter of his interlocking thoughts. The image was the rumpled figure of McQueen.

McQueen sat very still in his cell. With an almost mystical intensity, he was thinking himself beyond the enmeshing smell of urine mixed with disinfectant that had always for him meant prison. He had a method for doing this. He recreated in his mind big houses he had seen. This one was a big detached white house with a semi-circular balcony on the first floor. It faced the sea-front of an Ayrshire coastal town. Sometimes in McQueen's head they were hard to get into. This one had been easy. He put shaving foam on the burglar alarm and forced the kitchen window.

McQueen landed on his stockinged feet on the kitchen floor. His shoes were on the draining board. He tied their specially long laces together and hung them round his neck. He listened. His eyes became accustomed to the darkness. Something brushed against his leg and he almost called out. It was a cat. McQueen bent down and stroked it gently. He straightened and looked slowly round the kitchen. The kitchen was well appointed, rich in the shining surfaces of affluence. It glowed dimly like the entrance to Ali Baba's cave.

McQueen moved without sound towards the hall. He was wondering what he would find.

6

Homecoming

'Going home,' she said.
    'Graithnock,' she said.
'London,' she said.
'Frances Ritchie,' she said.

She treated his questions like spaces in an official form, impersonally, never digressing into humanising irrelevance. I am a stranger on a train, she was saying. She asked him nothing in return.

But the man was persistent. He had come on at Dumfries, entering a coach clogged with the boredom of several hours' travel, the unfinished crosswords, the empty whisky miniatures interred in their plastic cups, the crumpled beer cans rattling minutely to the motion of the train. Picking his way among the preoccupied stares and the occasionally stretched legs, he had sat down opposite Fran. The seats had only just been vacated by a mother and a small girl who had made Fran wonder if her own desire for children was as deep as she told herself it was.

His persistence wasn't offensive. It had none of the I-secretly-know-what-you-want-and-need machismo which Fran had learned to recognise from a distance like a waving flag and which caused her to shoot on sight. His persistence was gentle, slightly vulnerable, as if he had decided – for no reason that she could understand – that he wanted to please her. Although it was a smoker, he asked if she minded him smoking.

'Just thought I'd check,' he said. 'The way it's going these days, they'll be issuing a leper's bell with every packet.'

Her smile disappeared like a mistake being erased.

'So what took you from Graithnock to London?'

She looked out of the window. Would she have known that countryside was Scotland if the stations they passed through hadn't told her?

'The train,' she said. 'The 12.10 I think it was.'

The sharpness of her remark made her glance towards his silence. He was smiling.

'You gave some extra information there,' he said. 'Does that mean you're softening towards me?'

'I wouldn't bet on it,' she said.

But she was laughing. She noticed he had a smile as open as a blank cheque. In spite of herself, she felt the moment put down roots and blossom into one of those sudden intimacies between strangers. He discovered that she was a journalist. He claimed to have seen her by-line. ('That's what you call it? Isn't it? A by-line?') He convinced her by getting the newspaper right. He was a Further Education lecturer in English at Jordanhill College in Glasgow. He had been on a visit to students in Dumfries.

'I prefer taking the train when I can,' he said. 'You go by car, it's just a chore, isn't it? This way, you can turn it into a carnival. Watch. Just answer one question, that's all we need. What do you drink?'

He came back from the buffet with two gins and two cans of tonic for her, two whiskies and a plastic cupful of water for himself. They made a party between them. As with all good parties, the conversation went into overdrive.

'The new Glasgow?' he said. 'Looks like backdoor Thatcherism to me. What difference is it making to the people in the housing-schemes? How many investors invest for the good of others? That kind of investment's the Trojan

Horse, isn't it? Oh, look, these nice punters are giving us a prezzy. Let's bring it into the city. Then, when it's dark, its belly opens and they all come out to loot and pillage.'

'I think maybe *Manhattan*,' she said. 'But it's not exactly an easy choice. I still love *Play it again, Sam*, that scene where the hairdrier almost blows him away. I just think he's great. Who was it said that? Bette Midler? "You want to take him home and burp him."'

'Maybe I just haven't found the man,' she said. 'You volunteering? I'm involved at the moment, actually. But I don't think marriage is exactly imminent.'

'It's interesting enough,' she said. 'But you go to a lot of places without really seeing them. Because you're there for one purpose. It can be like travelling in a tunnel.'

'Oh, that was the worst time,' he said. 'Don't worry about it. Divorce? I can see what Dr Crippen was getting at. I'm not saying I agree with him. But murder must be a lot less hassle.'

Before the buffet closed ('Haven't we been lucky?' he said. 'They usually shut it about Carlisle but the fella in the buffet's drunk.'), she went and fetched them two more drinks. By the time they were drawing into Graithnock she had his telephone number (but he didn't have hers) and Fran was about to say goodbye to Tom.

Departure heightened their sense of closeness. He was helping her with her case and threatening to come with her since he felt it only right, considering how far they were along the road to marriage, that he should meet her parents. Just before he opened the door for her, he kissed her on the cheek.

Then she was on the platform with her case beside her and he was leaning out, waving with mock drama, and she felt slightly dazed with alcohol and elation, as if she were taking part in a scene from a film in which she might be the heroine and didn't know what would happen next, and then she turned and saw her parents.

75

They were standing thirty yards away, waiting for her to notice them. They would be doing that – not for them the spontaneity of running towards her. Victor and Agnes Ritchie, informal as a letterhead. They stood slightly apart, her father with his clipped, grey military moustache, a general in the army of the genteel, her mother with that expression some unknown experience had pickled on her face countless years ago. Fran wondered again how they had acquired their ability to turn joy to a dead thing at a touch and how they had managed to pass the gift on to her. Years of hopelessness they had taught her resurfaced in her at once. She suspected the value of the pleasure she had just had.

Her life in miniature, she thought, this journey. A promise something in her wouldn't allow her to fulfil. She didn't think she would be phoning him. She hoped she would but, standing there, she would have bet against it. She felt her faith in life and living evaporate. Her parents had taught her well. Maybe home is simply where you can't get away from, she thought.

As she lifted her case and walked towards them, she fingered the return ticket in the pocket of her jacket, wondering how far she would have to go finally to get away from here.

7

At the bar

The pub was quiet. When the big man with the ill-fitting suit came in, the barman noticed him more than he normally would have done. The suit was slightly out of fashion yet looked quite new and it was too big for him. He could have come back to it after a long illness. Yet it wasn't that either. Whatever had happened to him had tightened him but not diminished him. The charcoal grey cloth sat on him loosely but that looked like the suit's problem. You wouldn't have fancied whoever the suit might fit to come against the man who wore it.

He came up to the bar and seemed uncertain about what to order. He looked along the gantry with a bemused innocence, like a small boy in a sweet-shop.

'Sir?' the barman said.

The big man sighed and shook his head and took his time. His face looked as if it had just come off a whetstone. The cheek-bones were sharp, the mouth was taut. The eyes were preoccupied with their own thoughts. His pallor suggested a plant kept out of the light. Prison, the barman thought.

'Uh-huh,' the big man said. 'Fine day. I'll have.' It seemed a momentous choice. 'A pint of heavy.'

He watched the barman pull it. Paying, he took a small wad of singles from his pocket and fingered them

77

deliberately. He studied his change carefully. Then he retreated inside himself.

Making sure the patch of bar in front of him was clean, he spread his *Daily Record* on it and started to read, the sports pages first. His beer seemed to be for moistening his lips.

Before turning back to the television, the barman checked the pub in his quick but careful way. The afternoon was boringly in place. Old Dave and Sal were over to his left, beside the Space Invader. As usual, they were staring past each other. Dave was nursing half-an-inch of beer and Sal had only the lemon left from her gin and tonic, her thin lips working against each other endlessly, crocheting silence. That should be them till they went home for their tea. At the other end of the bar, Barney, the retired schoolteacher, was doing *The Times* crossword. Did he ever finish it? In the light from the window his half-pint looked as stale as cold tea.

The only other person in the pub was someone the barman didn't like. He had started to come in lately. Denim-dressed, he looked nasty-hard, a broad pitted face framed in long black hair. He was a fidgety drinker, one of those who keep looking over both shoulders as if they know somebody must be trying to take a liberty and they're determined to catch him at it. Just now, standing at the bar, he kept glancing along at the big man and seemed annoyed to get no reaction. His eyes were a demonstration looking for a place to happen. He took his pint like a penance.

The television was showing some kind of afternoon chat-show, two men talking who made the pub seem interesting. Each question sounded boring until you heard the answer and that made you want another question very quick. The barman was relieved to see Old Dave come towards the bar as if he was walking across America. It would be good if he made it before he died.

'Yes, Dave,' the barman said to encourage his progress. 'Another drink? What is this? Your anniversary?'

The barman noticed the big man had the paper open at page three. He knew what the man was seeing, having studied her this morning, a dark-haired girl called Minette with breasts like two separate states. But the big man wasn't looking at her so much as he was reading her, like a long novel. Then he flicked over to the front page, glanced, sipped his beer till it was an inch down the glass and went to the lavatory.

'Same again,' Dave said, having arrived. 'Tae hell wi' it. Ye're only young once.'

The barman laughed and turned his back on him. He had to cut more lemon. He had to find one of the lemons the pub had started getting in specially for Sal. After brief puzzlement, he did. He cut it carefully. He filled out gin, found ice, added the lemon. He turned back, put the drink on the counter, pulled a pint. As he laid the pint beside the gin and opened the tonic, pouring it, he noticed something in among the activity that bothered him. He suddenly realised what it was. The big man's pint-dish held nothing but traces of froth.

The barman was about to speak to the hard-faced man in denim when the big man walked back from the lavatory to the bar. His arrival froze the barman. The big man made to touch his paper, paused. He looked at his empty pint.

'Excuse me,' he said to the barman. 'Ah had a pint there.'

The moment crackled like an electrical storm. Even Old Dave got the message. His purse hung in his hand. He stared at the counter. The barman was wincing.

'That's right,' the man in denim said. 'Ye had a pint. But Ah drank it.'

The silence prolonged itself like an empty street with a man at either end of it. The barman knew that nobody else could interfere.

'Sorry?' the big man said.

'Ye had a pint, right enough. But Ah felt like it. So Ah drank it. That's the dinky-dory.'

So that was the story. The big man stared and lowered his eyes, looked up and smiled. It wasn't convincing. Nonchalant surrender never is. But he was doing his best to make it look as if it was.

'Oh, look,' he said. 'What does it matter? Ah can afford another one. Forget it.'

The barman was grateful but contemptuous. He didn't want trouble but he wouldn't have liked to go to sleep in the big man's head. And when the big man spoke again, he could hardly believe it.

'Look. If you need a drink, let me buy you another one. Come on. Give the man a pint of heavy.'

The barman felt as if he was pouring out the big man's blood but he did it. It was his job to keep the peace. The man in denim lifted the pint, winked at the barman.

'Cheers,' he said to the big man, smiling at him. 'Your good health. You obviously value it.'

He hadn't managed his first mouthful before the side of the big man's clenched right hand had hit the base of the glass like a demolition-ball. There was a splintered scream among the shards of exploding glass and the volleying beer.

Not unused to fast violence, the barman was stunned. The big man picked up his paper. He laid the price of a pint on the counter and nodded to the barman.

'If he's lookin' for me,' he said, 'the name's Rafferty. Cheerio. Nice shop you run.'

He went out. Lifting a dish-towel, the barman hurried round the counter and gave it to the man in denim. While he held his face together with it and the cloth saturated instantly with blood and he kept moaning, the barman found his first coherent reaction to the situation.

'You're barred,' he said.

8

In the steps of Spartacus

B enny Mullen had dogs. It wasn't that he deliberately
kept dogs or bought them or reared them. They were
a periodic manifestation in his life, like acne in teenagers.
Every so often he developed a dog.

Perhaps the condition wasn't unrelated to the fact that
he had become a widower in his early thirties. His wife,
Noreen, had encouraged him to acknowledge the helpless
compassion that was hidden at the centre of his nature and
he still felt it, like internal lesions. Maybe dogs could sniff
it out. He certainly couldn't explain their affinity for him.
They seemed to attach themselves to him from time to time
without warning.

One night when he came out of the pictures feeling
particularly aggressive (it had been a Clint Eastwood film),
he got on a bus with the one-dimensional purpose of coming
home. But by the time he stepped off the bus, he realised
he had a dog. He thought maybe it had been waiting in the
darkness near the bus-stop. The first time he had been
aware of it was when it was padding unconcernedly beside
him. He stopped. It stopped. He walked on. It walked on.
It might have been trained to obey him.

It was a smooth-haired fox terrier. It stayed with him for
some time, long enough to eat two corners of the hearth-rug
that Noreen hadn't liked much anyway (she had been
threatening to get a new one before she died) and the leg of

a kitchen chair, as well as quite a lot of more pedestrian fare. And it was gone as suddenly as it had come.

It ran away one evening in pursuit of a big mongrel bitch. The last Benny saw of it, it seemed to be closing the gap at the corner of the street. But maybe it didn't catch up until much later. It may have been so far away by the time it caught up with the bitch that the obvious thing was to follow somebody else home. It may have done that. It was that kind of dog.

Benny took its absence philosophically. For a week or so after that, he would rise at odd intervals of an evening and go outside. Moving around vaguely, he would call 'Billy Boy' (a name he had chosen for his own sectarian purposes and to which the dog seemed to answer as well as any other) or whistle absent-mindedly now and again. That dog didn't turn up but others did from time to time.

That was why when Fin Barclay walked into 'The Akimbo Arms' with the Greyhound, Benny felt justified in regarding himself as an expert on dogs.

You didn't have to be an expert to realise that it wasn't Mick the Miller Fin had on the leash. 'Bisto' (as Fin proudly announced – 'but that's no' its racin' name') was a kind of off-purple in colour, slightly hairy to be convincing as a greyhound and too skinny to be convincing as anything else.

'What's its racin' name?' Gus McPhater said, contemplating Bisto over his pint of McEwan's while the dog wagged its tail placatively. 'Paraplegic?'

'Whoever knitted that,' Benny said, 'is colour-blind for starters.'

'And must've lost the pattern,' Gus said.

'That dog's got splay feet,' Benny said.

Fin patted Bisto's head and looked at Gus pleadingly, willing him to say something nice. Gus wasn't an insensitive man.

'Mind you, it's nicer than yon dog old Jock Murray had,'

he said. 'The wan everybody just called "Scabby". That was a *really* ugly dog.'

Benny Mullen rose solemnly and walked round Bisto while the dog danced nervously, trying to keep its eyes on him. He felt its haunches and then pursed his lips. He made a couple of mystic passes down its forelegs. He stood up straight and stared at it. Fin was silent, awaiting the decision.

'You was robbed,' Benny said.

'I like it,' Fin said, 'I like it,' repetitively buffing up his dream of owning a greyhound. Benny's breath was clouding it.

'If ye got that dog for nothin',' Benny said, 'ye should ask for yer money back. You was robbed.'

The dog had started to attract the attention of others in the bar. Big Harry the barman was leaning over the counter to get a better view. As usual, his face was as happy as a death-mask.

'No dogs allowed in the bar, Fin,' he said. 'But you're in the clear wi' that.'

There was general laughter. Gus and Benny looked at each other. Kind people called Fin naïve. Unkind people didn't. But he was their friend. Something would have to be done.

Early the following evening Benny and Fin and Bisto were approaching a tenement in an old part of the town. Bisto, seeming to recognise the area, was straining at the leash. Fin was letting himself be pulled along.

'This the one?' Benny said.

'He's a nice man,' Fin said.

'Uh-huh. He's that nice maybe this time he'll sell ye a motor wi' no wheels.'

The flat was on the first floor. Benny ignored the bell, preferring the primitive authority of a triple knock on the door. It was opened by a small middle-aged woman who, like the room that was visible behind her at the end of the short hallway, shone with cleanness.

'Hullo, son. Bisto.'

The dog had a small fit of happiness. As the woman calmed Bisto down with the laying on of hands, she looked up enquiringly. Fin said nothing.

'Missus,' Benny said. 'Don't be alarmed. It's yer man we're here to see. Ah'd like a word with him.'

The woman looked as alarmed as a grandmother at a sewing-bee.

'Certainly, boys,' she said. 'Come in and sit yerselves down. Ah'm just making Davie's tea. He should be about five minutes. He's workin' a wee bit late the night. Would yese like somethin' yerselves?'

'We've had wur tea,' Benny said.

'Well,' Fin was saying.

'Some extra sausage here, son. Would ye like a piece on sausage?'

'That would be lovely, Mrs Brunton.'

'What about you, sir?'

'No thank you, m'dear,' Benny said, keeping things on a strictly business footing.

He watched with some distaste as Fin enjoyed his sandwich and a cup of tea. They didn't have long to wait.

Davie Brunton wasn't any taller than his wife. Benny, bulking big in the armchair, watched him.

'Hullo, hullo,' the small man said to everybody and crossed and unselfconsciously kissed his wife on the cheek. He wrestled briefly with Bisto. 'That you eatin' ma tea?'

Fin was beginning to explain how he came to be eating the sandwich when Davie Brunton ruffled his hair and told him not to be daft.

'With ye in a minute, boys,' he said. 'Just gi'e the face a wash.' He went through to the kitchen. 'Something good the night, Betty?'

'It's yer steak and sausage.'

'Ah married a wee genius.'

He came back through, stripped to his vest and towelling himself.

'Well, boys, what can Ah do ye for? You're no' havin' problems with the animal, are ye, son?'

'Ah think the problem's yours, sir,' Benny said.

Davie Brunton's eyes widened. He thoughtfully finished drying his arms and his hands. He threw the towel on a chair.

'Come again,' he said.

'It's just like this,' Benny said. 'You will give that boy his money back or you will have to perform.'

Davie Brunton nodded

'Uh-huh,' he said. He crossed the living-room and closed the door. 'Well, we'll just perform right now. On yer feet.'

Benny seemed to have forgotten his script. He saw the instant ignition into anger in the small man's eyes. He noticed the ominous bulge of his biceps. He looked at his wife. She was laying the table.

'Now wait a minute, sir,' Benny said. 'Let's not be hasty here. We're here to talk.'

'Naw,' Davie Brunton said. 'You're here tae listen. Get your fat arse out that chair or shut yer mouth.'

'Davie!'

'Ah'm all right, Betty. You come into a man's house an' threaten 'im? Are you a Martian? Silence. Ah'll tell you when to leave.'

He turned to Fin.

'Ah'm sorry, Mr Brunton –'

'Not your problem, son. Ah know what happened here. Ah was weaned on to solids quite a while ago. You happy wi' the dog, son?'

'Definitely.'

'Then you keep the dog.'

He crossed to the sideboard, opened a drawer, took something out. He came back to Fin.

'Here. There's your money back.'

'No, no, Mr Brunton. Ah couldn't –'

'It's yours, son. But you give a penny of it to that big man an' Ah'll take it out yer hide. That's a promise, son. Fin? That's what ye said it was, right? Ah like you, Fin. That's why ye've got the dog. You come back anytime. On yer own. An', Fin, son. That's a good dog ye've got. A tenement's no place for a grew, that's why Ah got rid of it.' He was stroking Bisto. 'Ah know, son. Ah know ye're fast. You'll show them. An' you.' He nodded at Benny. 'You ever see me in the street, you imitate auld Bisto here. Have it away on yer toes.'

He smiled suddenly, released the dog.

'Okay, gentlemen. The door's this way.'

By the time news of the meeting with Davie Brunton reached Gus McPhater, it had become the story of how effectively he had dispelled any doubts about Bisto's quality. His eloquence, it seemed, had been utterly convincing. Gus decided to put his claims to the test. The test was Mickey Andrews, the nearest thing Graithnock had to an *Encyclopaedia Britannica* of dogs.

In a big field near the Bringan, while a high wind thrashed the trees, rough measurements were made. Bisto was held by Benny Mullen. In the distance Fin Barclay hallooed. Bisto was released. Mickey pressed his stop-watch on release, pressed his stop-watch on arrival. The process was repeated eight times without comment from Mickey, while the others argued unavailingly for an interim report. After the eighth run, Mickey spoke.

'Your dog,' he said, 'is fast. Your dog is very, very fast.'

The dancing merriment of the others was surveyed bemusedly by Mickey, as if he were an adult at a children's party. When he spoke again, he killed the laughter suddenly, like someone bursting their balloon.

'Behave yerselves,' he said. 'Ye think fast is everythin'?'

'What else is there like?' Benny said.

'What about trappin'?' Mickey said. 'An' cornerin'? An' no' turnin' the heid. How often has this dog run before? An' where?'

Nobody knew.

'Still,' Benny said. 'It's maybe worth a try. Ah've got an idea.'

The others waited.

'Unfold yer plan, wee guru,' Gus said.

'Ye wouldny imagine,' Mickey said, studying Bisto, 'there could be another grew like him in Ayrshire. But there is. Auld Bisto's got a double or as near as dammit. Dick Raymond's dog, Nell's Joy. Nell's Joy? Nell must be a masochist. If ye strapped a lighted match to yon dug's nose, it couldny run fast enough to put it oot. Ye followin' so far?'

'Ah'm with ye, captain,' Gus said. 'Over an' out. But we don't want to run it wi' a name like Nell's Joy. What kinda name is that?'

'What difference does it make? As long as ye get the price on it.'

'We want oor own name for it.'

'Call it what ye like in yer heid.'

'Aye, right enough,' Gus said. 'As long as we know what its real name is.'

'So will Ah go an' see Dick Raymond?'

There were noddings all round. Fin Barclay was ecstatic and his joy transferred to Bisto, who seemed already to have developed an inordinate affection for Fin.

'Sh!' Gus said. 'We don't go at this like a cock at a grozet.'

'A grozet?' Fin asked.

'A gooseberry, Fin,' Gus said. 'A gooseberry. Ye see, names matter. Ask any boy called Marmaduke if they don't. The ancients used to believe names had magic in them. They imparted a quality to the thing named.'

'Ah like Bisto,' Fin said.

'Ah quite like Bisto as a flavourin' for ma mince as well, Fin. But it's not a name for our dog.'

Fin was delighted by the use of 'our'.

'This isn't just a dog, ye see. It's a wee chariot of dreams. When it runs at Thornbank, it'll be carryin' more than a hap wi' a number on its back. It'll be carryin' the hope of a better future for all of us. It needs a name that fits it.'

The moment had become the ceremony of the naming of the dog. Gus's brain needed a fresh pint of McEwan's for the purpose. They all stared at the dog while it nuzzled Fin's hand playfully, like an infant innocent of the fact that kingship awaits him.

'How about,' Benny said, 'Samurai?'

'They never ran in their lives,' Gus said.

'Casanova?' Benny suggested.

'You want it nuzzlin' every bitch on the way round?'

'Brownie?'

'Not quite what we're lookin' for, Fin. But this is.'

Gus rewarded himself with a drink from his pint. He stared at the dog.

'Spartacus,' he said. 'The hero of the working man.'

The other two said nothing.

'Trust me, boys,' Gus said. 'It's Spartacus.'

On the night, they were all there. Dick Raymond duly put Spartacus, alias Nell's Joy, in for the third race. The two hundred and ten pounds they had gathered deviously as stake money was divided among Mickey, Dick, Benny and Gus, Mickey getting the extra tenner. They bided their time, moved in on the bookmakers simultaneously. The prices were good, ranging from seven-to-one to five-to-one. As they waited for the race to begin, they felt as if they were waiting to receive a joint inheritance.

The trapping was no problem. Spartacus came out the box like something fired from a cannon. He made a yard in the first thirty. He flowed round the first bend like quicksilver with a hap on it. The longer they ran the further he was ahead. As he came round the last bend into the home straight, the other dogs were a diminishing cloud behind him.

Five mouths were screaming triumph that suddenly stuck in their throats. For Spartacus, approaching them, slowed to a lollop. They realised with horror that he was looking for a face in the crowd. While the other dogs swept past him in a knot of confused endeavour, Spartacus put his paws on the fence and barked happily into Fin's face, waiting for appreciation of how well he had done.

'Ah'm just thinkin',' Gus said.

'Whar's that?' Benny said.

'Ah got the name wrong,' Gus said.

'How's that?' Benny said.

'Spartacus. Know what he did, Benny? He led a rebellion that brought Rome to its knees. Then when he had the city at his mercy, he turned back and went to Sicily. His home, like. They killed him there. It was the wrong name.'

'We could always change the name. We would have tae, after that last carry-on.'

'And maybe if Fin didn't come with us to the track.'

They both nodded. They had all finished eating the cheese sandwiches Benny had brought with him and finished drinking Gus's flask-tea. Gus and Benny were lying in bright sunshine in the hilly part of a field while below them Fin was playing with Spartacus, the homing greyhound. In the happy plenitude of such moments a burp can taste of profundity and maybe mayflies hallucinate eternity.

9

Sentences

The way the grey-haired man came into the room, its location might have been Mars and not Edinburgh. He waited just inside the door for several moments, using the area like a decompression chamber. He was looking round uncertainly. All there was to see was an old Victorian bar, reflective with wood, and a few customers scattered round it. There were two people behind the oval counter, a young man and an older woman. The young man had a face so smug he could have been feeling sorry for the rest of the world that it wasn't him. The older woman was looking at the young man as if she might be agreeing with him. They were chatting.

The grey-haired man moved. He walked with a diffidence that belied his appearance. He looked vaguely military. He wore a beautifully laundered blue-checked shirt, a tie that could have been knotted by computer and a navy cashmere sweater. His fawn trousers had a crease that suggested he had never sat down in them. The brown brogues were highly polished. He had a carefully·clipped moustache and his hair was neatly cut. He carried in his left hand what looked like a large black envelope. It was a fine plastic raincoat, folded and held in a perspex pouch. It was a day of particular heat, of cloudless sky.

The grey-haired man walked tentatively round the entire oval of the bar. His glances indicated that he was looking for someone. They were glances too quick to be registering much, furtive as a camera shutter. They were a means not of seeing who was there, merely who wasn't. The young man was following the walk round the bar with his eyes without stopping talking. The grey-haired man came back to the point inside the door where he had been and he hesitated again. He was deciding something.

He crossed to the bar. He waited. The young barman must have stopped watching the grey-haired man, for he made no move. The grey-haired man waited. The woman behind the bar looked up at him. As she made to move, the barman put his hand on her arm without looking round. He winked at her and finished what he was saying and turned slowly and walked along the bar.

'Thought you were just sight-seeing,' he said.

The grey-haired man laughed. The barman didn't.

'A gin and tonic,' the grey-haired man said. The barman was turning away. 'And –'

The barman turned back towards him.

'And a vodka and lemonade. Both with ice.'

The barman made a performance of looking to see if there were someone behind the grey-haired man.

'Sorry?'

'A gin and tonic and a vodka and lemonade. Both with ice.'

The barman shrugged. While he mixed the drinks, the grey-haired man looked at his watch. When the drinks came, the grey-haired man paid and lifted the glasses and paused again. There was no seating at the bar but there were tables positioned away from the counter. Most of them were empty. The grey-haired man chose the table nearest the door. He sat down and set aside the vodka and lemonade and began to sip the gin and tonic.

Two girls came in, their accents announcing them as American as the door opened. They looked about twenty, one wearing jeans and a tee-shirt, the other a shirt and a long wrap-around skirt. Their eager exchange seemed to consist mainly of names like Degas and Renoir and Pissarro. They hit the muted atmosphere of the bar like a carnival in a graveyard. They had marvellously vivid and open faces, as if the light from the Statue of Liberty were illuminating them from within. The barman was waiting for them at the counter by the time they arrived.

'Yes, ladies. What can we do you for?'

'Two beers, please,' the blonde one said. She smiled absently and her mouth appeared to have enough large and perfect teeth to provide an extra set for someone else.

'Beers?' the barman said archly.

The girls noticed him.

'Beers? For ladies of your obvious sophistication?'

'We're slumming today,' the dark-haired one said. 'You got lager?'

'Indeed we have. I take it you mean halves?'

'Yeah. Glasses of beer,' the dark-haired one said.

While he was getting the drinks, the barman continued to talk to them, asking what they had seen and where they had come from. Twice he said, 'Yeah.' The girls made polite responses without seriously interrupting their conversation. Still preoccupied with painters, they sat down on the nearest available seats, which happened to be at the same table as the grey-haired man. 'Hi,' the blonde girl said to him and they went on talking to each other.

A smile had occurred like a spasm on the grey-haired man's face when the blonde girl spoke to him. The spasm became a general nervousness. His eyes were unable to find a place where they could comfortably rest. He fidgeted a lot.

Suddenly he stood up, lifting both glasses and, awkwardly, his plastic raincoat. He crossed quickly and sat down at another table. The dark-haired girl glanced across at him and made a face of incomprehension to her friend. The table the grey-haired man had chosen was beside another long table with two men there, one at each end of it. The grey-haired man made as if to get up again and then subsided.

Neither of the two men acknowledged the grey-haired man's sudden shift of position. They were obviously not together. One of them was reading a book. He had a pint on the table in front of him. The other man was turning a beer-mat ruminatively in his fingers. He looked like someone trying to commit its texture to memory. His glass of whisky and water shone in one spear of moted sunlight from the window behind him, like a holy object in a Hollywood film.

The grey-haired man looked at his watch again. His gin and tonic was more than half-full but he gulped it down, the unmelted ice rattling against his teeth. He rose and crossed to the bar surprisingly quickly. The barman and the woman were busy talking and the grey-haired man moved round the counter until he was in the barman's line of vision. He held up his glass.

'Same again?' the barman said.

'Yes, please,' the grey-haired man said.

He was watching the door. When the barman brought him a gin and tonic and a vodka and lemonade, the grey-haired man pulled back his hand, which was holding a pound note.

'Oh,' he said.

'What?' the barman said.

'Sorry. Nothing.'

The grey-haired man took more money from his pocket and paid for the drinks and brought them back to his table. He sat looking at the two vodkas with lemonade and the gin and tonic. He took the first vodka and lemonade he had bought and started to drink it. He didn't seem to be enjoying it but in three swallows it was finished. He got up and put the glass on the bar beside the woman. He put the glass down noisily, so that the woman turned round and saw it and started to wash it. He came and sat down and arranged the two remaining glasses on the table in front of him. He did it with the deliberation of someone dressing a window, putting his head to the side to look at it.

A woman came into the bar. She was already past middle age but still attractive. Her body was slightly heavy without being unshapely. Her face had a confidence that gave it an unsagging definition. The grey-haired man was already making to get up and waving to her but she had seen him at once and came towards his table.

'Agnes!' he called unnecessarily.

'I thought you'd wait outside,' she said.

'I didn't know how much longer you would be.'

'What difference does that make?'

'I've only just come in.'

'I hope you haven't been drinking.'

The grey-haired man indicated the two full glasses on his table.

'I was waiting for *you*,' he said.

He stood up to pull out a chair for her. She glanced at the two men at the next table.

'Not here,' she said. 'Bring the drinks.'

She walked to a table that was well away from anyone else and sat down. The grey-haired man followed her with the drinks, his plastic raincoat held clumsily under one arm.

The man with the book looked up. He stared at the back of the grey-haired man as he went away careful not to spill any of the drink. The man with the beer-mat was watching too. They turned towards each other.

The man with the book exhaled incredulity.

'I wonder how long he's been putting up with that?'

The man with the beer-mat shook his head.

'You would hope not long,' he said. 'But maybe that stuff's very ageing. Maybe he's only twenty-five.'

They smiled at each other and withdrew into their separate camps of disbelief. They didn't know that thirty-two years, five months and nine days previously the grey-haired man had been found by his wife in the living-room of their house with his hand up the dress of the woman from next door and had received no remission of sentence for good conduct.

10

Getting along

Margaret and John Hislop had one of those marriages where there wasn't room to swing an ego. All was mutual justice and consideration and fairness. He only golfed between the hours of two and six on a Sunday because that was when she visited her mother. Her night-class was always on a Tuesday, regardless of what was available then, for that was when he worked late. Both watched television programmes which were neither's favourite. They didn't have arguments, they had discussions. It was a marriage made by a committee and each day passed like a stifled yawn. It was as if the family crypt had been ordered early and they were living in it.

Then she saw him where he wasn't supposed to be and he had another woman with him and the marriage ended. It did not end immediately. They had half-hearted discussions when she seemed to be looking at him through her fingers. Something was dead in her. They expended a lot of breath but it was like trying to give the kiss of life to a corpse. He went to the other woman, who seemed to her unattractively brash (Margaret had demanded a meeting) and, what was most hurtful to her, older.

The settlement was fine. She was able to buy a nice apartment and she had the furniture. She still had her job and she had money in the bank. She went out occasionally with other men for a while.

But she could not forgive them. She could not forgive the world and the world did not mind. It passed her window indifferently in sports cars and couples with prams and buses full of preoccupied faces.

The apartment became the only significant terrain of her life. She had rubber plants and tiger plants and potted flowers. She took up painting by numbers. She read a lot, mainly improbable romances. She prepared for years of working around her house like a woman patiently sitting down to sew her own shroud.

II

Mick's day

It is Tuesday, not that it matters. The calendar is what
other people follow, like an observance Mick Haggerty
used to practise but has lost faith in. For Mick, most
days come anonymous, without distinguishing features of
purpose or appointment.

In any week only one time has constant individuality:
Monday when he goes to the Post Office to collect the money
on his Social Security book. It is the only money he is ever
guaranteed to have. Sometimes in the pub, mainly on a
Friday or a Saturday, an evening will enlarge into almost a
kind of party, an echo of the times when he was earning.
(Earlier this year, a local man home from Toronto, remembering Mick's generosity when he was working, and aware
of how things are with him now, slipped him a tenner.) But
there is no way to foretell these times. For the most part,
the names of the days are irrelevant.

But this is Tuesday. He wakens and reckons the morning
is fairly well on. Sleeping late is one way to postpone having
to confront the day. Doing that means going to bed late so
that he won't surface too early. This is not a room he likes
to lie awake in. Its bleakness works on the mind like a
battery for recharging your depression.

The permanently drawn curtains are admitting enough
daylight to light the room. The wallpaper beside his bed
shows the familiar patches of pink below the peeled sections

of floral, landmarks for his consciousness. The floor is bare boards with one small piece of carpet on them. Besides the bed, the furniture is two chairs. One of them is a battered easy chair for holding his clothes. The other is a wickerwork chair on which the ashtray sits, with a week of ash and cigarette-stubs in it.

He has no cigarettes but that isn't important. He has developed an intermittent style of smoking. He occasionally buys a ten-pack of Benson and Hedges and usually only smokes if he is having a drink and sometimes not even then. When he is offered a cigarette, he tends to alternate one acceptance with several refusals, perhaps maintaining his hold on a habit he can't well afford or perhaps measuring the charity he'll accept.

He gets up and dresses. He had thought of changing his shirt but the only clean one he has left is a green shirt someone gave him and his Protestant origins in Feeney near Londonderry make him sometimes a little reluctant to put it on.

He goes through to the living-room where the only time-piece in the house, an old alarm clock, lies face-down on the mantelpiece. If you don't keep it lying face-down, it stops ticking. It is ten past ten. He looks into the other bedroom to check that Old Freddie is all right.

Old Freddie mutters vaguely in acknowledgement of his presence. Freddie is in his early seventies and he has had a rough night. He usually does on a Monday, for that is when Mick pays him his £8 rent from the Social Security money. Freddie can't handle the drink the way he used to. The operation that gave him a bag where his bladder should be can't be helping.

Mick comes back through to the living-room. Its furniture echoes the kind of furniture in the bedroom: bare floorboards with a few pieces of carpet, a battered sideboard and three beat-up chairs and a raddled settee. There is an old wireless. They had a second-hand television but it went on the blink.

They have lived in this house for a year now. Mick doesn't like it as much as the first house. He has had digs with Old Freddie for twelve years, ever since Mick's marriage broke up after sixteen years. 'It just didn't work,' Mick says. At least there were no children who would suffer. For about a year after that he lived in a Model Lodging House, long since demolished. Then Freddie offered him digs. For a time in the other house Freddie's sister lived with them. She was separated from her husband, a miner who had gone to Nottingham to look for work. Even after she rejoined her husband, the house seemed to retain a little of her touch. Mick feels that a house where there isn't a woman never gets to feel quite right.

He goes through to the kitchen. He and Freddie buy their food separately, keep it in separate cupboards. They find that is the best way to try and make the money last. But if either of them runs short of food, it is an agreement that he can share the other's. Mick makes himself two fried eggs, a slice of bread and butter and a cup of tea.

When he has eaten, he goes to the lavatory. He washes himself in cold water. He comes through to the living-room, puts on his jacket and collects his library books. He may go to the public library two or three times a week. Before leaving the house, he looks in on Old Freddie again.

Outside, it is cold but not raining. One of the bleakest urban prospects you will see is a run-down council housing-scheme. All such architecture ever has to commend it is freshness. When that goes, there is not the residual shabby impressiveness of Victorian buildings, like an old actor rather grandly down on his luck. There is only grey rough-cast stained with weather, overgrown gardens, a flotsam of rubbish left when the tide of respectability receded.

Mick's street is mainly like that. The council has refurbished a few houses, adding red-brick porches to the front. But the majority of the houses are the architectural equivalent of a huddle of winos. Some have been boarded up. Grass grows through the flagstones of the pavement in some places. From the scale of the dog-turds that aren't uncommon on the pavement, it wouldn't take an Indian scout to work out that the dogs around here tend to come in big sizes. One or two can be seen almost at any time of the day, mooching vaguely around as now, as if they too were on the dole. A big black dog is reading the pavement with its nose. From time to time it lifts its leg and squirts like an aerosol, adding its own comment.

Mick is heading towards the park as his shortest way to the town centre. His route takes him past the rubble of a recently demolished block of old flats towards a vast empty area already cleared. Men appear to be testing the ground there, presumably for rebuilding. On his left is a lemonade-making factory not long shut down. A few of its windows are broken and a door hangs open. He knows three sisters not much younger than himself who never married and who had worked in that place since they left school.

Mick himself is fifty-seven now. It is four years since he worked. There have been times, he says, when he could lose one job and find another in the same day. Since he came from Ireland to Glasgow (where he lived for three years) when he was eighteen, he has worked in a flour mill, in an engineering works, on hydro-electric schemes but mainly in the building trade. He was proud of his reputation as a good worker. He was never given to saving, knowing there would always be another job. Then, four years ago, there wasn't. There still isn't. He should know, he says. He has been looking.

When he arrives at the pedestrian precinct in the town centre, he joins some men he knows who are lounging there. The desultory talk among them is about the horses and the dogs and who's done what and to whom and where there might be a job going.

Mick wonders briefly about going along to the Job Centre and decides against it. It's a bit like having your own uselessness officially confirmed. He used to go there a lot but the regularity of failure becomes harder to take, not easier. And every year that passes makes work for him less likely. 'It's hard enough for men in their forties,' he says. 'They don't want you when you're my age.'

Mick leaves the men in the precinct and goes to the Public Library. There's a nice girl there who knows him by name now. His favourite books are detective stories and cowboy stories. But he reads more or less anything. One of the books he really enjoyed was by a man named Leonard Woolf. He thinks it was called *The Village in the Jungle*. Today he picks three cowboy books: *Max Brand's Best Western Stories*, *Trask and The Mark of Kane* and *Manhunter*.

When he comes out, the temptation is to go to the pub. But if he goes to the pub, the danger is that he will stay there, nursing pints till it closes. This is only Tuesday. If he exhausts his money now, it will be a long way to the next oasis. He walks back home.

Old Freddie is still in his bed. He isn't feeling talkative. Mick comes through to the living-room and starts half-heartedly reading *Max Brand's Best Western Stories*. He doesn't like reading so much during the day. His best time for reading is late at night and in the early hours of the morning. Old Freddie is coughing.

The drinking doesn't agree with Freddie any more, if it ever did. It is perhaps a good thing that he no longer has his redundancy money. When he was paid off, he was offered £30 a month or a small lump sum. Freddie chose the lump sum and had liquefied his assets, as it were, within a year. But he had some good nights.

Mick finally goes to the pub in late afternoon. The pub is the focal point of his life. It is companionship, unofficial social work department and cabaret. Everybody knows him. If he is struggling, quite a few people there are prepared to stand him a drink. It is an understandable indulgence because any time Mick has money he isn't against buying a drink for someone else.

In the pub, too, both the owners and the customers have been known to help Mick out. He may get a pub-meal for free. Someone may bring him in a winter anorak. He may get the offer of a few hours' gardening. It's that kind of pub, a talking shop rich in anecdote where most of the people who go are well-known to one another. Perhaps people don't mind helping Mick because he is remarkably unself-pitying and unembittered about his situation. If he ever falls out with anyone, it is usually in a righteous cause.

He has more than a touch of the Galahads in his nature. One night in the pub Mick saw a woman being annoyed by a man. Mick decided to adminster chastisement. But the man unsportingly moved and Mick's fist connected with the woman's forehead: damsel in deeper distress. But she understood the chivalry of the intention and proceeded to wear the lump like a Burton diamond. (Perhaps the moral is that when a drunk Irishman comes to a lady's aid, her trouble may only be starting.)

Tonight Mick stays till the pub shuts and comes out mellow but not, he feels, drunk. There is in the park, between him and home, a flight of earth steps buttressed with wood. The height between steps is uneven. Mick is in the habit of using them to gauge his condition, like a blood sample. Tonight the alcohol count isn't high.

When he gets home, Freddie is in the living-room. He has eaten and gone out but he hasn't had much to drink. Mick makes himself roasted cheese on two slices of bread and a cup of tea. He usually eats more than he has eaten today, his favourite food being liver.

Freddie doesn't want anything but they sit and talk as Mick eats. They mention Freddie's sister, who died in Nottingham. They talk again about whether Mick will ever go back to Feeney. Mick can't see it happening, since he would hardly know anyone there any more.

When Freddie goes to bed, Mick picks up *Trask And The*

Mark Of Kane. The street is quiet. He hunkers down into his personal situation, bothering no one.

But the more time that passes like this, the less capable Mick is likely to become of ever getting out of his present helpless condition. Time never merely passes. It defines us as it goes until we run out of potential to contradict what it tells us. Mick's situation is like a prison sentence without any crime committed. It is an indeterminate sentence. So far he has served four years.

12

Tig

When they barred Mickey Andrews from 'The Narrow Place', they did a bad thing. 'The Narrow Place' was a one-room bar, one entrance, one exit. It had been named by Big Fergie, the owner, presumably from a sepulchral sense of humour, since he had been told it meant the grave. It was a gantry, a counter, a piece of worn linoleum to stand on and one continuous red leather bench seat along the wall, pockmarked with cigarette burns. The Cairo Hilton it wasn't. So where did Big Fergie get off barring anybody from there in the first place?

He did it on a Thursday night after the dogs. If there had been no dogs, there would have been no 'Narrow Place'. The dog-track at Thornbank was a flapping track, which meant that it was unofficial, not subject to the rules of the National Greyhound Racing Council. Interesting things happened there. The markings on a particular black and white dog might change subtly from one week to the next. A dog that had appeared to be running through molasses for three weeks in a row would suddenly look to be in danger of catching the hare. These things were a puzzle and a mystery to many.

But every Tuesday and Thursday night the many came and tried to solve the mystery once again. One of the many was Mickey Andrews. He was a small man of a mainly pleasant disposition. The central preoccupation of his life was animals. Around the edges of this preoccupation Mickey had almost absent-mindedly acquired a wife and three daughters. The three girls were married and Sadie, his wife, had long ago learned to find her own preoccupations, which included her grandchildren, bingo and television soap operas.

Mickey's preoccupations might have seemed less varied than Sadie's, but only to an outsider. As many animals as there were, so many animals was Mickey interested in. Apart from his interest in all kinds of domestic animals, he watched any television programme he could find about nature. He speculated philosophically about many aspects of the natural world: for example, which would win in a straight contest – a crocodile or a shark? Or what is, pound for pound, the most ferocious creature on earth? Mickey's main bet was on the wolverine, with a side-bet on a Pyrenean rodent , called a desman, which he had seen on a David Attenborough programme. A wolverine was, in Mickey's assessment, a set of champing teeth with fur round it.

Mickey loved all animals, fierce or gentle. 'Their nature's their nature,' he sometimes said cryptically. As with all true lovers, love gave him knowledge of the beloved. People with pets in the Graithnock housing development where he lived came to him with their problems. They weren't always well received.

Once a woman came to Mickey's door with a toy poodle which was wearing what looked like a small but rather expensive fur coat. The dog, the woman said, was pining. The first sign that Mickey's diagnosis wasn't favourable was that he didn't ask her in. He stared at the dog which was fidgeting on his doorstep.

Mickey loved all animals but there was a kind of hierarchy to his love and the toy poodle did not occupy a high place in it. He had once described a toy poodle as 'a sandwich for an alsatian'.

'Yes,' he said to the woman. 'Your dog's got a problem.'

'What is it?' she asked.

'You.'

The woman stared at him.

'Missus,' he said. 'Its legs are bucklin' under that thing on its back. What's that for? Dogs've got coats already. How'd *you* like two skins? Ye'd suffocate. Yer dog's pinin' right enough. It's pinin' for an owner with a brain.'

And he closed the door. For Mickey wanted animals to be animals. He hated human sentimentality to be superimposed on the animal world. 'Give them their own natures,' he sometimes said cryptically. And, 'When an animal dies, it dies.' And, 'You ever see a canary die? Just draps aff the perch. Doesny phone a doctor. No relatives round the bed.' Mickey hated people who had birthday parties for dogs or sent Christmas cards with pawmarks on them. But his love of animals was real. It was a love for the animals, not his idea of them. It was a love so unmistakable that a friend had once referred to him as St Francis of Assisi. Yet Mickey had characteristics St Francis appears not to have had. One of them was irrational anger.

It was the anger that led to his being barred from 'The Narrow Place'. That Thursday Mickey had gone to Thornbank greyhound track. Every Tuesday and Thursday he did that. Those nights were the highlight of his week.

Each night came in two parts. There was the session at the stadium with the heraldry of the greyhounds parading on the green turf and racing under the lights, the frosted breath of the onlookers rising up into the air like prayers. There was the session in the pub afterwards.

'The Narrow Place' was, more than any other place, where Mickey found his social fulfilment. Every Tuesday and Thursday night it was packed. As far as takings went, Big Fergie could afford to forget the rest of the week. Men and greyhounds crammed themselves in, in apparent defiance of the physical possibilities. The talk was all of dogs and who was trying and who wasn't and how best to prepare a dog for a race. Among these men Mickey was a king. He knew more about the dogs than anyone else. More importantly, he was among people who, no matter how dubious their motives, acknowledged two nights a week the beauty and grace and importance of greyhounds and, by implication, of animals. It was as close as Mickey got to a place of worship. He couldn't imagine not going there – until that Thursday night.

Mickey was arguing pleasantly with a big man from Thornbank. Mickey liked arguing. 'Arguing's like monkey-gland steak,' he sometimes said cryptically. But he had never said this to the big man. The big man was not getting angry but he was not getting any happier. They were arguing about judging greyhounds just by looking at them and, while the big man remained unconvinced by Mickey's reasoning, everybody else within earshot was obviously starting to side with Mickey. The big man couldn't help feeling that people were agreeing with Mickey not because he was right but because he often said things with a pleasing neatness, or a displeasing neatness, if you were the big man. He decided that Mickey was not taking the argument very seriously and he thought that he might as well do the same. That was when the big man did something foolish. He knocked off Mickey's cap.

No one who knew Mickey Andrews well would have knocked off his cap. No one with any sensitivity to the mysteriousness of others would knock off anyone's cap. Who knows where the nuclear buttons are in a stranger's nature? Mickey's cap was like an integral part of himself. He wore it in the house as well as outside. Even friends never saw him without it. Rumour had it that he went to bed with it on. When the big man knocked it off Mickey's head, everyone could see why Mickey wore it.

With his cap off, Mickey instantly aged about twenty years. He had thick curly hair at the sides of his head and at the back, still only slightly grey. The entire upper part of his head shone like a glass eye in the cheap fluorescent light of Big Fergie's bar. The effect of knocking Mickey's cap off was similar to taking the cork off the bottle of an evil genie.

Mickey became a blur of malice. He caught his cap in mid-air and pulled it back on his head and, simultaneously it seemed, punched the big man in the mouth. So tight with people was 'The Narrow Place' on a dog night that an incident became in seconds a riot. Much noisy confusion and falling about ensued. Dogs barked and men wrestled with leashes. Oaths were heard. People dreaded they might suffocate. Some struggled cravenly towards the door like passengers who think the ship is sinking. All this took up much time. When comparative silence was at last restored by Big Fergie, there was some damage to glasses and one dog had a cut paw and the room was murmuring with vague threats. But Mickey's cap had remained miraculously on his head.

A summary hearing was held. Numerous claims for compensation for spilled beer were brusquely dismissed by Big Fergie. There was only one serious issue here. How had this started? Who was to blame? The evidence, like a forest of fingers, pointed at Mickey. It was useless for him to plead his case. There was no way he could present it effectively. The very core of his defence, the exceptional importance of the cap as a part of his identity, was the very thing he couldn't admit. It would have been equivalent to preserving his propriety by stripping naked. Without the admission of this crucial extenuating circumstance, Big Fergie ruled that a punch in the mouth was in no way a just response to getting your cap playfully knocked off. The verdict was final. Mickey was barred.

Mickey protested. When had he ever caused trouble before? For how many years had he been Big Fergie's customer? How many Tuesday or Thursday nights had he missed that Fergie could remember? And, pathetically enough (even Mickey felt it), he hadn't finished his pint.

Big Fergie took Mickey's glass with the remains of his pint in it, opened one half of the double doors and threw the beer into the street. He handed the glass to someone else. He held the door open.

'Your beer's out there,' he said. 'You want it, follow it.'

Mickey looked at Big Fergie. He knew Big Fergie was jealous of him. Too many times Mickey had shown Big Fergie's pronouncements about greyhounds to be rubbish, the undigested scraps of other men's knowledge heard over the counter. Nonsense talked at the pitch of your voice was still nonsense. But what chance did you have accusing the judge to his face of corruption?

Still Mickey couldn't step out the door. To cross that line was to abandon the most purely pleasurable place of meeting he had in his life. What would he do without it? How could he leave? Big Fergie solved his problem for him. He took Mickey by the shoulder with his free hand and flung him out. The door closed behind him.

Mickey came back at the door as if he had been on elastic. His pride was outraged. But with one hand on each of the brass handles of the double doors, he halted. A counter-charge of pride went through him like an electric shock. He wouldn't be begging. They could keep their pub. But this wasn't over. Somehow Big Fergie would pay for this. Somehow he would pay. Mickey went home.

Throughout the next few days Mickey brooded. Sadie was aware of the difference in him but, after a few unsuccessful enquiries, she left him to deal with it. She knew that Mickey believed in what he called 'men's business'. It meant that there were areas of their lives that were primarily his concern. Just as he wouldn't dare to advise Sadie on how to cook whatever meal she gave him, so if a grizzly bear came to the door, he wouldn't ask her to answer it. He would take care of the bad things. This appeared to be one of them.

During the weekend the usual sort of visitors came and

went, bringing their small problems. Mrs Wallace's bud-
gerigar needed to have its claws clipped. Old Stan Baird
brought his pet rabbit Dusky, an animal Mickey had previously suggested couldn't have been much older than Stan
himself. Stan was worried about Dusky. No wonder. Running his hands over it expertly, Mickey said gently, 'What
we've got here is a growth with a rabbit attached.' Brutus,
Danny Park's alsatian, was showing the first signs of distem-
per. A small tear-stained girl turned up with a goldfish
floating in a goldfish bowl. A lot of people believed in
Mickey Andrews.

Mickey gave everybody an audience but he did it absently, in the manner of Solomon solving other people's
problems while conducting an internal argument with God.
Sadie knew that whatever had been worrying him was
continuing to worry him. It was Monday evening before
Mickey came in from his hut in the back garden with a
less troubled expression on his face. It was an interesting
expression. It wasn't happy, exactly. It was more an expression of calm and intense concentration, like someone
who is trying to see through walls.

Mickey put a piece of wood on the mantelpiece and sat
down and stared at it. Sadie glanced up from watching
television. It was an ordinary-looking piece of wood. It was
about a foot long, two inches wide and an inch-and-a-half
thick. Mickey had obviously been planing it smooth. Sadie
knew the rules of the game Mickey was playing and when
she spoke she didn't expect an answer.

'That's lovely, Mickey,' she said. 'But d'ye think it'll ever
catch on?'

Mickey smiled. After ten minutes' further contemplation,
he took the piece of wood and went back out to his hut.
When he returned and replaced the piece of wood on the
mantelpiece, Sadie looked up again. Mickey had bored two
holes, one at each end of the wood. From each hole, knotted
so that it held firm, dangled a two-foot length of rope.

'My,' Sadie said. 'Ye're a wonder. Only you would've seen that's exactly what was needed.'

Mickey smiled. Quite a few people missed him at the Thornbank dogs on Tuesday night and commented on his absence. The comments extended into 'The Narrow Place'. There was a lot of talk about him. Some felt that he shouldn't have been barred. The big man who had been punched on the mouth was one of the leading voices in presenting Mickey's appeal. Being punched by Mickey, he said, was like being assaulted with a ping-pong ball. But Big Fergie wouldn't waver. Mickey Andrews was barred.

It was then, as magically as if their talk had conjured him, that Mickey appeared. He stood in the doorway of the bar, holding open one of the double doors. The pub seemed even busier than usual, perhaps in expectation of a sequel to the barring of Mickey Andrews, and it took some time for everybody in the bar to realise that Mickey was there. But the talk subsided piecemeal until everyone in the place was craning and staring to see Mickey Andrews. The bar was as quiet as a Western street at sun-up. Mickey was staring steadily at Big Fergie. Big Fergie was staring steadily at Mickey.

'You meant it?' Mickey said. 'That Ah'm barred?'

'Ah meant it. You're barred.'

'For how long then?'

'How long you got to live?'

'You mean for life?'

'You're barred for life. And if you get reincarnated, try to remember that.'

'Okay,' Mickey said. 'Just thought Ah'd check,' and he took from inside his jacket Dusky, the cancer-ridden rabbit which Old Stan had finally asked him to have put down.

'Die nobly, friend,' Mickey muttered to Dusky. 'It's comin' to us all.' And then, remembering the old childhood game, he shouted to Big Fergie, 'Tig! You're het,' as he threw the rabbit into the bar.

It landed on a man's shoulder and hopped onto the bar. It seemed to have a new and spectacular life that enabled it, however briefly, to outrun its cancer.

Mickey saw it jump from the counter on to the gantry area, scattering glasses and bottles, as Big Fergie swore, as dogs leaped and barked, twanging their leashes, as men fell and glasses broke, as the noise reached panic-stricken crescendo, as Mickey closed the door and rammed home the piece of wood he had taken from his pocket and tied the ropes in a quadruple knot round the double door-handles and walked off down the empty street.

13

Beached

There was one yacht's sail out in the bay, sickled with wind stress, a cipher of all the journeys she would never make. The beach was almost empty. As Marion shook sand from the towel, she paused. The moment held her like a freeze-frame in a film. Beyond the preoccupations of the moment, she studied where she really was.

The sky predominated, surrounded her in a vivid air that she felt lucid with loss. The clouds offered no certain shapes. They appeared to her lost purposes that loitered round the thought of what they might have been, a house, a bridge, a map of a country where she might have gone. Involuntarily, she held the towel to her, the comfort-rag a child can't bear to part with.

The sea was grey. The day was almost over. And she was held again in that moment where near gold of an afternoon converts to lead, recurrent mood of life's failed alchemy.

The beach was littered with sought pleasure. A burst beach-ball lay abandoned. A Coca-Cola bottle was embedded in the sand. An empty plastic bag was imitating tumbleweed. She saw an afternoon as archaeology.

She could see the figure of a child haloed against the sky in the distance. She couldn't make out whether it was a boy or a girl. It seemed caught in a dancing prism of light. She couldn't tell whether the child was advancing or receding.

In the middle distance was the centre-piece. They were

a young man and a girl. Whatever was trivial in them couldn't be seen from this softening distance, in this poignant light. Their shapes moved her like an ancient hieroglyph, a rune of passion. Their leant heads seemed a brave conspiracy against everything around them.

They looked so vulnerable she almost wanted to cry out to them but she understood it would be like crying out to herself, shouting a warning to a past self who couldn't hear. They were where she had once been and would never be again.

An inexpressible nostalgia that seemed as vast as the sky tremored through her and earthed itself in the practicalities at her feet. She bent and collected Michael's wet and abandoned trunks, Lucy's discarded sun-hat. Holding the beach-bag in one hand and gathering up the debris of their day with the other, she seemed to see herself from above, how eccentrically isolated her life had become. She saw herself doubled over like an old woman scrabbling after sticks, the little pieces of identity that would fuel her sense of herself. The small actions, seemingly incidental, defined her identity. They reminded her that Harry was dead and that a part of her would never be quite as alive again. There was hope, of course, but it was a smaller hope.

And yet the passion in her for living was undiminished. It was simply that it had learned it had no permanent home. Her experience had taught her that. It was as if, psychologically, she would live the rest of her life in a tent. This momentary scene was one of that passion's temporary houses.

The faces of the children blotted it out. Michael was impatient to be going. Lucy pressed in on her with the word that she was hungry. Instinctively, she embraced them both, hoarding the profit of her loss. They squirmed a little as if embarrassed but she held on to them. She knew that the moment was only a family on a beach getting ready to go home but she also knew that it was more. She knew that what she saw over their heads was just a widow's stare but she also knew that the child and the couple and the yacht were a promise life had made to her a while ago, a promise only fully known in its departure.

She clung to her lonely vision even as it faded, a primitive painting she had made herself from colours that couldn't survive the corroding salt sea air, mixed crudely on some palette of the heart.

14

How many miles to Babylon?

'Benny!' Matt O'Neill shouted up through cupped hands. 'Benny Mullen!'

In a moment, a broad, close-cropped head appeared, projecting beyond the uncompleted upper edge of the building, like a blueprint for a gargoyle. The wide mouth spouted words.

'What the hell is it?'

'Time up, Benny,' Matt O'Neill called up. 'Ah'm sendin' yer taxi for ye.'

He worked the pulley, and the wooden platform on its chains, normally used as a hoist for building materials, rose steadily till it stopped at the level where Benny was working. Benny had disappeared.

'Watch this,' Matt O'Neill said.

'That's Tank's job,' Johnny Rayburn said.

'Tank's job! Got a boy of ten could do it. Goin' to give Benny a wee thrill here.'

'You watch what ye're doin'.'

Matt was smiling.

'It'll be just like the Big Dipper. Benny says he can't remember bein' frightened. Should be no problem for a man of his calibre.'

He pronounced it jocularly, to rhyme with 'Khyber'. Wanting no part of it, Johnny Rayburn found a barrow that needed shifting but didn't shift it to where he couldn't see what was happening. Benny reappeared with his jacket over his shoulder and stepped out casually, maybe fifty feet above them, on to the platform, his free hand taking hold of one of the vertical chains. The platform started to descend smoothly with Benny gazing down upon them. Then Matt suddenly spun the pulley. The platform dropped sheer for about fifteen feet before Matt braked it dead. They could hear Benny bouncing on the wooden platform, and muffled cursing among the dancing rattle of the chains, and the worn work jacket, emptily bulbuous at the pockets where Benny always carried his eight slices of bread and cheese, floated like an empty parachute to the ground. Benny's head came over the edge of the platform and said, 'Ya bastard! Wait till Ah get doon there.'

Matt was laughing helplessly.

'Ye'll need to be more polite than that, Benny, if ye want to get doon,' he said.

He was still laughing when he felt a grip manacle almost his entire forearm. He looked into a stare like burnished metal.

'What's the game?' Tank Anderson said.

'It's a bit of fun.'

'You're the only one that's laughin'.'

'Maybe Ah'm the only one wi' a sense of humour.'

'Ah've seen a man killed in one of these,' Tank said. 'You lose control of this, ye've got a man wearin' his pelvis for a hat. Ya bastard. Benny! You okay?'

'Okay, Tank.'

'You wait there till this man comes doon,' Tank muttered.

'That'll worry me,' Matt said.

Tank reset the pulley gently into motion. A few of the men had gathered to see what would happen. As the platform reached ground level, they could see how shaken Benny was. 'Okay' had been an attitude adopted, not a fact. Benny's face was trying to find an expression of hardness but the expression floated somehow uneasily on his features, wouldn't gell. Johnny had picked up his jacket and offered it to him. But Benny stepped off the platform and walked past him to face Matt O'Neill.

'Wait a minute, Benny,' Tank said and, spinning on his heel, hit Matt O'Neill on the jaw with a hand clenched into a club.

Matt sprawled among a pile of stone chips as if he was going to drown in them. He surfaced and spat a couple of chips. Tank had turned to Benny.

'Ah'm site foreman, Benny,' he said. 'It was ma instruction Matt ignored. So it's ma responsibility. And it's finished. Okay?'

Benny nodded. Tank crossed and held out his open hand towards Matt. Matt hesitated only briefly, for the hand extended to him had a local legend on the end of it. He clasped his hand in Tank's and Tank hauled him erect.

'Better than losin' yer job,' Tank said and winked.

'Aye, ye've had yer chips, Matt,' somebody said.

The laughter was a general amnesty. Tank brought Matt and Benny together to shake hands. Benny grimaced as they shook.

'That bloody chain,' he said.

He showed the palm of his hand, bruised where the chain of the platform had gnashed on it.

'Ah'm glad ye don't shake with yer jaw,' Matt said and rubbed his chin.

The crisis shared and averted developed a temporary camaraderie among them, like a small war survived with no serious casualties. Six of them made a little parade to 'The Market Bar'. Benny wasn't a regular there. He drank in 'The Akimbo Arms'. Usually he split off from the men and went there alone after his work. But tonight he felt himself part of them. He had been the centre of a small event and he innocently assumed that was what made them more than normally friendly towards him. It didn't occur to him that it was because they had seen him momentarily divested of the tough image he wore like a suit of armour. The fear floating on his face as he stepped off the platform had allowed him into their company. Their jokes were the admission charge.

'Bet that's cured yer constipation, Benny,' Johnny Rayburn said as they worked on their first pints.

His bowels were one of the site topics, like the government.

'You still as bad?' Deke Dawson asked.

'Ye kiddin'?' Frank Climie said. 'Ye could hire out Benny's arse for nestin'. A bird could rear a brood up there between performances.'

'It's all the cheese sandwiches ye eat,' Tank was suggesting.

The pub became busy. As the banter flew around him seeming, under the transforming effect of four pints of heavy beer on his growling stomach, like exotically coloured birds in a noisy aviary, Benny had a visionary experience. He didn't have them often. This one began in a slow, congealing realisation, a still point glowing in his mind like a steady light. He could have been killed. If Matt O'Neill's hand had slipped, if the pulley had snapped under the sudden pressure, if the brake hadn't held . . . he could have been killed.

He looked at Matt O'Neill nodding to Deke Dawson and laughing into his pint, and Benny felt not anger or a desire for revenge but a strange shivering thrill which his body contained comfortably like an overcoat, an overcoat he was still wearing. He saw Matt not with malice but with something oddly like gratitude, saw those very banal features take on a significance beyond themselves, as if Matt were a messenger from a dark force. The message was the grandeur of ordinary life. The warmth of the pub, the middle-aged barmaid's back bulging sensuously in two places beneath the strap of her brassière, the uninhibited laughter of a man at the end of the bar, a whorl of smoke unravelling in air, the found gold that formed in a whisky-glass held to an optic, all were gifts of pleasure. They demanded a bigger expression of gratitude than he had been giving them. He needed a gesture.

Then he saw it, a sign the expansiveness of his own mood had created. A man beside him had the *Evening Times* half-folded on the bar. The headline seemed to point at Benny: The Flying Scots. The photograph beneath it showed three men at Glasgow Airport smiling self-consciously for the camera. They were flying out to Saudi Arabia. The story talked about the strangeness of modern life where workers caught a plane instead of a tram to go to their work. There was a reference to their wives waiting with rolling-pins if their wages were short when they got back. It occurred to Benny sadly that he wouldn't have had that problem. But the idea struck him like a revelation. The world was a small place. What need did he have to spend his life here? What reason did he have for staying? Time was running out. He didn't want to waken up at sixty and regret what he hadn't done. He was going to travel.

Like a sudden convert to the generous possibilities of life, he bought another round of drinks and included the man with the *Evening Times*, despite his embarrassed prot-estations. He slapped Matt O'Neill mystifyingly on the shoulder, as if he had saved his life instead of almost ending it. He said, 'Aye, Tank by name and Tank by nature', so many times that Tank said, 'Actually, ma name's Harry'. He bought a carry-out of eight cans of export and had to be followed out of the pub by Johnny Rayburn because he had left them behind. Swinging the cans in their plastic bag as he walked, he brought his new dream up the road with him, singing 'Scotland the Brave' quietly to himself.

The house was a place he didn't like entering in the early evening. It wasn't so bad late at night because he had usually taken enough beer by then to numb the pain. But this evening was all right. Painlessness had come early. The

thought that this council house was too big for him didn't
settle its gloom around him as it normally did, didn't echo
with the ghosts of the children he had wanted as if it were
a castle rented for a clan that hadn't turned up, Mullen's
Folly. He went through and dropped his jacket on the
double-bed without noticing particularly how empty it
looked. He still moved among dead dreams but already it
was as if he had found something that for the moment was
a small, if ludicrous, compensation, a dream of his own, a
miraculous by-blow, like an illegitimate grandchild where
there had been no children.

He still spent the evening almost entirely in the living-
room, though. It was the room that was the nearest thing
to home he had. It was where Noreen and he had always
sat. Sometimes, when the loneliness was bad, he even slept
here, buttoning up the heavy army-style coat Noreen had
bought for him in Milletts' Stores and dossing down in front
of the coal fire both of them had agreed they would never
change. On these occasions, the vague impulse in him was
that by not sleeping alone in the bed he wasn't endorsing
the fact of her death, as if he had a say in it.

Tonight he had first left the living-room to go into the
kitchen and put on two pork chops and then had come back
through and drunk three cans of export, talking loudly to
himself as had become his habit, and waited till the smell
of the chops announced that they were burnt. He had
salvaged some charred pieces of meat and chewed them into
threads which he washed down with more export.

Having obeyed in his own way one of the several warnings
that Noreen had handed down to him as her stoutness
dematerialised relentlessly from leukaemia ('See that you eat
right'), he went on with the preferred part of his private
communion, the drink. He chatted to the room like
company. It was his favourite place for talking to himself,
the only part of the house he felt furnished with his presence.
The rest of it he couldn't afford psychologically to maintain.

'A close call right enough,' he said. 'It fairly makes ye think.'

He thought of Noreen. There had been no early warning system for her. Once they knew what she had, they knew what would happen. No chance to rethink their lives, no time significantly to make the most of what was left. The nature of the illness had meant that they couldn't. The best they had managed was the week in Morecambe after one of the treatments had given her a temporary boost. They had taken a room in a big hotel, at his insistence. He had wanted to take her everywhere, give her everything. But they had been like a one-legged man trying to dance. She had retained all her bantering warmth but instead of its enlarging him, as it had done before, he had shrivelled before it. He caught her looking at him secretly, looks that knew how lost he would be, and he had felt her receding from him and he was colder that week of hot weather than he had ever been before, like being slowly skinned. That week he had spent longer in the lavatory than at any other time. The men on the site might have found that funny. But he had needed a place to cry without being seen.

The conjured presence of Noreen made him admit the truth of himself, as it always did. She was the one who had found him out. She had provided a home for Benny's secret softness, a place where he could take off his muscles and let his shameful gentleness emerge. He might fool the citizenry with his deliberate swagger and the haircut that made his hair look like moss on a cannonball, but Noreen hadn't believed him. It was as if she had known him when he went first to the orphanage at the age of ten, very thin and with a bird-like capacity for panic.

Always frightened of feeling before, he had found himself after her death with a great load of affection like stolen goods and nowhere to fence it. He had started again to stash it in his muscles and hope that nobody would notice. Glancing drunkenly around the room, he saw it looking like a gymnasium. He had a bullworker leaning in a corner, a chest expander fixed to the door and assorted weights in the cupboard. It was as if he had been trying to intimidate his grief.

But to his sense of her he admitted the truth again. He couldn't quite believe in himself as a hard man. He had watched nearly every Clint Eastwood film several times, like taking a course in callousness, but somehow the treatment hadn't quite taken. No doubt he would go on trying, since out there he didn't know what else to do. Sitting in this room, however, he owned up to himself. He had been terrified on the platform. He had been glad when Tank Anderson settled the matter with Matt O'Neill, because Benny wasn't sure that he fancied his chances against Matt.

'A man's a man for a' that,' he said to his seventh can of export with his finger in the ring-pull.

The explosion of escaping gas was like faint applause. Benny loved Robert Burns, not just the poetry, which he could quote at great and sometimes pub-emptying length, but the man, the hard life, the democratic stance of him, the sense he gave of effortlessly incarnating Scottishness, the fact that he, like Benny, was an Ayrshireman. Scottishness was very important to Benny. He wasn't sure what it was but, whatever it was, it bit like lockjaw and the fever of it was in his blood. When he read Burns, he looked in a national mirror that told him who he was and forbade him to be diminished by what other people had. He was enough in himself. The greatest expression of his Scottishness that he could think of at the moment was to travel. It was what his heart told him to do.

> 'The hert's aye the pairt aye
> That maks us right or wrang.'

He would travel. He might even emigrate. Wasn't that what Scots did? He remembered a story he had heard.

Somebody in the pub had been talking about a book he was reading. It was about a man sailing round the world himself. That was something to do, except that Benny didn't know a gib-sail from a tablecloth. But the man had written a book about his trip. One place he stopped in South America, he met some natives and they told him about a primitive tribe up-country who had red hair. The man had visited them and, sure enough, they had dark skins and reddish hair. The man thought they were descendants of Scotsmen who had settled there. Panama, Benny thought it was. The idea of it made him shake his head in wonderment.

'Christ, we're everywhere,' Benny said, raising his beer-can in a toast to the empty room. 'We are the people. Open an alligator's gub in the Congo an' a Scotsman'll nod oot at ye. We're everywhere. Australia, Canada, America, South America, Asia.' He paused, running out of places. 'Russia. There was always Scotsmen in Russia. An' all over Europe. For centuries. India. A lotta Scottish graves in India.' He started to sing. 'There was a soldier, a Scottish soldier. We are the people. Scotsmen can go anywhere. An' why no' me? Why not Benny Mullen? Ye can go anywhere. Ye could even go –' His mind eddied with the drink and he waited to find what exotic flotsam it would throw up. 'To Babylon.' The word shimmered in his head. 'Babylon.' He laughed and drained his can. 'Correct. Ye could even go to Babylon. How many miles wid that be?'

His laughter was a celebration of how simple life was. His eighth can gave him his vision complete. He would go to Babylon, not necessarily to stay there. He would see it first and then decide. But it was a beginning. He would need an atlas.

He referred the project to his memory of Noreen, like praying at a shrine before a journey. He felt her approval given. As if an oracle had spoken, he remembered another of her parting warnings, given from her hospital bed when her body hardly made a bump on the coverlet and families were murmuring all around them in the ward and her eyes had rekindled for a moment into their old liveliness:

'You've a life to live, Benny Mullen. Live it! Ye're therty-five. Don't let me catch you skulkin' in coarners. Ah married a man, not a mouse.'

That had been three years ago and what had he done to justify her faith? He would do it now, for the two of them. He stood up suddenly.

'By Christ, ye're right, Noreen. You are right, ma bonny lass. An' say Ah've said it.'

He toasted himself with his can. It was empty. Wondering vaguely if there would still be a can left over in the fridge from his last carry-out, he made to move through there and slipped on an empty beercan. The can he was holding slithered across the floor. He landed on his hands and knees. He gave long thought to the problem of rising and slowly subsided on the carpet. He felt it was his first step on the way to Babylon. Trying to find a comfortable position for his right leg, he kicked another empty can. Just before he slept, doubts began to buzz like flies around his dying enthusiasm. How could he go? Where would the money come from? Would he feel the same in the morning? He hoped that Noreen would forgive him for the mess.

15

Callers

8.30 a.m. The phone rang in the sunlit room. At the third ring there was a click and a recorded message came on. In spite of the mechanical distortion, the woman's voice was warm. It had a quality of vulnerability, suggestive of beginning to surface out of sleep. It was a voice that had given some men from time to time a delicate and pleasurable spasm, as if they were having a gentle orgasm through the ear. Behind it, a record was playing somewhere. It was only just impossible to make out the tune.

The voice said: 'Hullo. This is Fran Ritchie. I'm sorry I'm not in. But I'm hithering and thithering quite a lot these days. The fact that I could say that proves I'm not drunk. Whoever you are, your message is welcome. I'll get back to you as soon as I can. Please wait for the horrible bleep.'

As the bleep came, a man's voice said, 'Shit.' The word was barely decipherable. The voice became irritably clear against a background noise of traffic. 'Fran. Mike. I need to see you. I know Polly's been phoning you. Before you went to Southend. She told me last night. Didn't sleep a wink. Jesus, some time I've had. Look. I had to tell her. The guilt was breaking my balls. You've got your other involvement, anyway. Don't deny it. I'm sorry she's taking some of it out on you. That wasn't my idea. But, believe me, you've got the best of it. You only have to listen to her

on the phone. And you can always put the phone down.
Me. I'm permanently plugged into her. And it's not just
words either. Know what happened last night? She beat me
up. One stage, she was pulling me up and down the floor
by my hair. Christ. My scalp feels as if it's been tenderised.
Another session like that and it'll be a Woolworth's wig for
me. I don't fancy going home tonight.' The voice stopped
talking. There were sounds that weren't clear. One could
have been tapping on glass. 'You've got to help me here,
Fran. We can synchronise our stories. Minimise the whole
thing. Polly says you refuse to tell her anything. Good girl
so far. But we have to meet and sort something out. Phone
me at the office. Soon as you can. Right? Fran, this thing
could destroy my children. You know how I feel about them.
You've always understood that. One last favour. That's all
I'm asking. Don't let me down. Otherwise, I'm going to
have to start up a refuge for battered husbands. If we –'
There were rapid pips on the line. 'Shit. No more money.
Phone me.'

8.45 a.m. The woman's voice that followed the bleep was
querulous, as if the empty room were letting her down.

'Oh no. Fran, it's Mum. Why didn't you phone? Especially after the day I had. Your father was utterly impossible. Those latest pills aren't helping at all. I might as well
give him smarties. I don't know how long I can cope with
this. You know what he wants to do now? He wants to
convert the attic. Can you imagine it? After all this time?
He wants to convert the attic. All the years I asked him to
do it. Now he decides. Now that he's developed five thumbs
on each hand. Now he's going to convert the attic. The
attic. He might as well want to explore Antarctica. I just
about had to chain myself to the pull-down ladder to stop
him. This can't go on. You know how much just letting him
hear your voice can help. Phone as soon as you get back.
And when you finally come up, remember the tin of walnut
oil.'

10.32 a.m. 'Hullo, Lucy's godmother. We trust you're remembering Sunday. Don't you dare be in Africa. Phone for final details. Love.'

11.47 a.m. 'I don't know how welcome this message will be, Fran. It's Donald Evans, your friendly neighbourhood bank manager. I'm sorry to be the bearer of bad tidings. But your £4,000 overdraft facility has become a five-and-a-half thousand pound monster. You'll have to come in. Talk we must. You simply can't go on like this. This is London, Fran. Not Disneyland. It's not monopoly money we're issuing. Phone me. Don't hide from it in your usual fey and charming way. Phone. Liked your last piece in the paper. The one about women in prison. Phone me.'

11.53 a.m. The woman's voice was not being allowed to go where it wanted, like a dog on a very tight leash. 'I've been trying to give you time to get out of bed. I imagine that usually takes a while for you. You never know who's going to be in there with you. Cow. You call yourself a journalist, I believe. I call you a whore. Don't worry. I'll be calling again. And again. See you in court.'

1.21 p.m. 'Fran. Mike. I'm sorry about the message this morning. Forgive a man whose hair's falling out. But don't hide, lovely. How long does it take to get back from Southend? Remember, no matter what happens, I'll always love you in my way. It may be a pretty crippled way but there we are. If you get back this afternoon, please phone me. I'll be in the office.'

3.59 p.m. The woman's voice spoke against one of Bach's violin concertos. It sounded like one of the strings. 'Fran. Susie here. Just to say thanks yet again. And give you a progress report. I'm fine. Annabel's fine. She loves the cottage. So do I. After the last few months, I'd forgotten there were places like this. The big bad wolf can't get to us here. He doesn't know where we are. I can hear my nerves begin to quieten down already. Listen. Annabel's beginning to talk. At least here, with just the two of us, her first words won't be swear words. It's all thanks to you. I've just canonised you. Saint Frances of Kentish Town. Trust me, Fran. I'll be paying back every penny. Must go. Annabel's eating some flowers. Catch you between your fascinating assignments. Love you.'

Five times, at 4.20 p.m., at 5.01 p.m., at 5.05 p.m., at 6.46 p.m., at 7.58 p.m., the telephone rang but each time the receiver was replaced at the other end before the recorded message had been completed.

8.50 p.m. 'Fran. I'm still waiting. And so is your father. If you get back before midnight, please phone us.'

9.05 p.m. 'The man you love to hate, Fran. What's going on? You met the man of your dreams in Southend? You must have small dreams. Interesting developments in connection with the Peterborough piece. I think you should do it. Phone me soonest. But not during the hours of darkness. Janice has rediscovered her nerves.'

9.32 p.m. 'Mike here. Mike. Remember me? Where are you? Why aren't you phoning? I've had about enough of this. I know who's behind it. Alan Martin. Right? The East End sophisticate. Your bit of rough trade. Thinks he's a hard man, does he? Tell him I know people could break his knee-caps just by looking at him. Tell him that. You phone me. I'm at –' A lot of voices invaded the phone. Someone was singing 'On the banks of the Wabash far away'. He came back on and very precisely stated a number. 'You phone me. D'you hear? Bloody well phone me.'

10.03 p.m. 'Cow. Slut. Whore. Cocksucker. Marriage-breaker. 'Bye.'

10.22 p.m. 'Hullo. Alan Martin here. This message is for Mike Thomas. Are you listening, bastard? Yes. I know your tricks. Fran's just told me. No. Don't try to stop me, love. He's got it coming. I know you've still got a key, Thomas. And I know you like listening to Fran's answering machine. Well, shove this up your ear-hole, shit-face. Fran's with me. And that's where she's staying. She's had enough of being nursemaid to a neurotic. She won't be coming back to the flat except to move her things. And I'll be with her. If you show face, you'll be wearing your bollocks for a cravat. End of message.'

10.44 p.m. 'Don't believe it. After I've done. Hope you're pleased with yourself. Children. You don't care about children. Godmother? Huh. Not over. Not yet. But thanks. Oh, thank you very much.'

The connection was sustained for sixty-four seconds in silence except for a muffled sound before the receiver was replaced.

11.13 p.m. 'Hullo, you. This is Eddie Kendrick. I feel I shouldn't have to say my name. But my parents taught me politeness. I think maybe they overdid it. Anyway, I can't quite trust you yet to know my voice. I couldn't take it if I was talking to you for five minutes and you couldn't work out who it was. So this is me. Eddie Kendrick. How are ye, love? Me, I'm walking on the moon. You know what I did today? I wrote the best pieces I've ever written. I know I have. All right. I'm quietly as drunk as a monkey. But it's the truth. It'll be in the paper tomorrow. You're the main person I want to read it. You remember the game of darts we had in 'The Popinjay'? I was at my boring worst that night. If they had a charge 'drunk in charge of a mouth', I would've got twenty years. Your tolerance was amazing. That's when it started for me. You treated me like a human being when I was an arsehole. I never forget it. Remember the big man who wanted to dance on my head. Had a point. You went right between us. I thought you were like Joan of Arc. Never forgot it. That's when it started for me. What I'm saying is. I don't exactly know. I've always liked your work. It's like an extension of your smile. Some smile. A motel sign in the desert. Okay. I better get the head out of overdrive. I want to celebrate. That's all. Just celebrate. That's what I'm asking. All those times since. In the pub. Talking about bye-lines and shit. I've just been thinking you. What I want to do. Is see you tomorrow night. I've taken a liberty here. I've booked a table for two at 'L'Escargot'. And let's see. We'll just see. The table's for half-past eight. And we meet in 'The Popinjay' at seven o'clock. Where it began. I'm a romantic's what I am. Violins in attendance. Okay? I'll phone you again tomorrow. Just come and we'll see. Be there, you. Sleep nice.'

The glow from the streetlamp outside made a path of light across the room, along which lay, like signposts on a journey, a magazine open at photographs of some exotic place, a lighter and a discarded pill bottle, which was empty.

16

End game

'Ah'm just thinkin', Jeanie,' Gus McPhater said, laying open on his knee his paperback copy of *The Essential Schopenhauer*. He had been leafing back and forwards through the section 'On Human Nature'.

'Oh yes,' Jeanie said. 'The doctor warned ye about that.'

Gus laughed loudly, seeming to suggest that being married to a witty woman was a joy forever. But Jeanie didn't respond. She was watching another of her old films on television, what she called 'a good romantic, old-fashioned picture, before they started showin' their knickers every two minutes'. This one was *The Greatest Show on Earth*.

It wasn't concentration on the film that had made her fail to respond. Just as Gus could read Schopenhauer while Betty Hutton was dancing on a trampoline and singing a song at the same time (amazing breath control, Gus thought over the edge of his book), so Jeanie could engage in quite elaborate conversation while watching a film. Once, Gus remembered, during *The Enchanted Cottage* she had argued scathingly for half-an-hour about the pointlessness of his tendency to read books that 'normal' people didn't understand. Gus had found her contempt rendered powerless against him because she had been simultaneously enthralled by a picture the main point of which was that a man who had been hideously disfigured in the war underwent instant plastic surgery when he crossed the threshold of an old cottage. While she watched her films, he read and they both talked during these activities, as if they had left their minds quietly knitting on their own.

It was for a different reason that Jeanie didn't react to the generosity of Gus's laughter. He had applied the water but the flower didn't open. She had learned to suspect Gus most when his approach was most casual. 'There's something, Jeanie,' he would say, or 'D'ye know what?' or 'Ah'm just thinkin',' and Jeanie's senses would quicken as if she had just spotted someone loitering with intent. Watching Charlton Heston (wasn't he a fine-looking big man?), she was waiting. Gus glanced back at Schopenhauer: 'Money, which represents all the good things of this world, and is these good things in the abstract . . .'

'Naw, but,' Gus said. 'Ah was just thinkin'. How long is it since you saw your Sadie?'

Under the appearance of following the action on the screen, Jeanie scouted the question carefully. She could see no ambush. Her sister Sadie lived in Toronto. That seemed a long way round to go to lay a trap.

'Must be five year,' Jeanie said.

'It must be. That's right. It's five year past since she came over wi' Big Tam.'

'He had put on an awful weight,' Jeanie said.

'Well, we're none of us gettin' any younger.'

'That's true.'

She had seen Charlton Heston in a disaster film recently and he had looked so much older. She had resented Gus asking if Charlton was the disaster. But he was looking his best in this one.

'Aye,' she said. 'Ah saw auld Sammy Pryce on Tuesday. Or was it Monday? No, it was Tuesday. For Ah remember Ah had just come oot the butcher's. And his face looks that sad these days. It's the saddest face Ah've ever seen.'

'That's just tired facial muscles. That's all it is. Makes everythin' sag. Sammy looks like a bloodhound.'

· Jeanie said nothing. She had little patience with the way Gus turned everything into a theory. She wasn't the only one who had noted that tendency. In 'The Akimbo Arms', where he drank, Gus McPhater was paid court to in a way that was only half-jocular. He had more than once declared himself to be in the tradition of the Scottish autodidacts. Even the word was typical. It was natural that he would prefer it to 'self-taught'. He would seldom say 'giraffe' when he could say 'camelopard'. It was that preference for fancy words that sometimes made people defensively try to out-manoeuvre him. But that wasn't an easy thing to do, for besides being well-read he could think fast on his feet or sitting down, which was the more usual posture. (He sometimes said he was a founder member of the peri-sedentary school of philosophy.)

Once in 'The Akimbo Arms' a group of students had turned up with what was obviously a prearranged plan to disconcert him. He had been handling himself well when the subject of Oscar Wilde was raised. One of the students had been studying him intensively at university. He noticed a certain vagueness pass across Gus's features.

'You know his stuff?' the student asked.

'Oscar Wilde?' Gus winked at the regulars in the bar.

'I'll bet you a pint you can't tell me one thing he said.'

Gus gazed at the ceiling.

'One thing Oscar Wilde said?'

'That's right.'

'Set up the pint,' Gus said to Harry the barman. 'If Ah win, you pay. If Ah lose, Ah pay. All right?'

The student agreed. Gus stared at the pint thoughtfully. He turned to the student.

'Good evening,' he said, and was drinking deep before the student realised that Gus was quoting.

That occasional hint of charlatanism was effectively offset by the things Gus genuinely knew. If somebody mentioned Esperanto, Gus could tell him that it had been invented by

Zamenhof and that he was a Pole. He could describe the flag of Zimbabwe. It was as if his early career as a merchant seaman had developed an imaginative extension. Once Jeanie's protestations had put him in dry-dock, as he expressed it, he had sent his mind travelling to exotic facts and imaginary landscapes. His theories were his rough maps of those inner territories. They were travellers' tales of the intellect and, as in most travellers' tales, truth was usually in there somewhere, though not always immediately recognisable.

Jeanie had long ago ceased to look for it. She simply waited for the theory of the moment to pass, like static on a radio. She had decided that Gus's theories never changed anything. They were something to be put up with. If you married somebody you knew liked garlic, you couldn't spend the rest of your life complaining about bad breath.

'But as Sammy is,' Gus said. 'So shall we be.'

On the television Cornel Wilde was talking in a funny accent to a woman. In this film he was always comparing women to drink. To this woman he was talking about 'shompanye'. Jeanie assumed he meant champagne.

'Time's runnin' out for us, too, Jeanie,' Gus was saying.

'We're only fifty-eight. Sammy's in his seventies.'

'Fifty-eight. Fifty-eight.' Gus said it with sonorous melancholy, like the tolling of a bell.

'You'll be fifty-nine in August,' Jeanie said.

'That's why we should do what we want to do while we can, Jeanie. Life's for livin'. Ye don't know what could happen to Sadie. Ye've never even been over there. You should go. What's to stop ye? The lassies are married. Ye've seen them settled. Enjoy yerself, wumman. Go to Canada.'

'How could Ah afford that?'

'Ye've yer wee bit money. Yer nest egg.'

At the mention of the money, Jeanie listened more carefully to him. Since she had won three-and-a-half thousand pounds on the football pools a year ago and put it in the bank, Gus had been referring to it in a variety of ways, as like someone looking for a password.

'And what would you be doin'?'

'Well, Ah could come along.' He paused. 'Ah miss the travel.' He paused. 'And maybe take in some other places while you're at Sadie's.'

Jeanie's head swivelled round from the television. She looked at him and nodded. It wasn't a friendly nod. She wasn't agreeing with him but with herself.

'Huh!' she said. 'A train through the Rockies.'

'Sorry?'

She was watching the television again.

'Ah think Ah've lost the thread o' this conversation,' Gus said.

'A train through the Rockies,' Jeanie said.

Gus knew what Jeanie meant. Jeanie knew that Gus knew what Jeanie meant. Gus knew that Jeanie knew that Gus knew what Jeanie meant.

'Ah don't know what ye're talkin' about,' Gus said.

Jeanie smiled. It was a smile it had taken years to temper, steely and impregnable. It was a fortress of a smile. Gus philosophically regretted, not for the first time, that law of diminishing returns in human relationships whereby what was given in intimacy came back malice. When they were younger, Gus's ambition to take a train through the Rockies, from Calgary to Vancouver, was a dream they had jocularly shared. Out of all the travelling he had done, that was the one thing he had quite wilfully decided he had missed. It had become somehow climactically important for him. If he had been Moses, a train through the Rockies would have been Canaan. 'When we're older,' Jeanie had often said. 'An' the weans are oot from oor feet.' He regretted his big mouth. If people didn't know your dreams, how could they thwart them?

'No train through the Rockies for you, ma lad,' Jeanie said. 'My Goad. You've wanted yer hands on that money since Ah won it. The one time in ma life Ah've had a few pounds by me. An' ye're slevering at the chops tae get yer hands on it.'

Gus glanced down at 'On Human Nature' as if he couldn't believe in it. He watched Jeanie watching television.

'That,' he said, 'is a contemptible remark. You should see about yerself, missus. Yer mind's poisoned. It's maybe all the radiation off that telly.'

Jeanie sat smugly saying nothing.

'But here the envious man finds himself in an unfortunate position; for all his blows fall powerless as soon as it is known that they come from him,' Schopenhauer said.

Gus's mind circled Jeanie's silence cautiously.

'What's the point of havin' money and doin' nothin' with it?'

'Ye never know what's round the corner.'

'Another bloody corner. Ye could go on like that till they bury it with ye.'

'We've one grandchild an' another on the way. There's always a place for money tae go.'

'Ah'll see them right. Ah'm earnin'.'

'A bookie's clerk!'

'Ah'm a marker. Ah mark up the prices.'

'That's the nearest you'll get tae money. Seein' other folk collect it. An' how long will ye be there?'

'How d'ye mean?'

'How many jobs have you had since ye came out the Merchant Navy?'

The question settled between them in the silence, as awesome in its unanswerability as the riddle of the universe. Gus half-heartedly started to count back and gave up. You might as well ask Casanova for a quick count of his ladies.

'Ah like to try different things,' he said.

'Ye should try work sometime.'

'Ah've always worked. And you've always had yer money.'

It was true, so Jeanie didn't answer. But a lot of other things were true as well, such as that he had always worked on his own terms, taking to every job he had ever had an intractable pride that he obeyed, regardless of the circumstances in which they were living. There was the time she had been pregnant with Donna, her second, and they were very short of money and he had walked into the house early in the afternoon. He had only just got the job as a storeman in a printer's warehouse. Once she had found out why he was home, her disbelief had lasted for four wordless days until he found another job. He had argued with the foreman about the number of islands in the Japanese archipelago and, impassioned beyond common sense, had finished up shouting that control of words should never be left in the hands of an ignoramus and that he couldn't work for a moron.

Jeanie had never known where the next bout of unemployment was coming from. The calendar had always been a financial minefield for her. She had sometimes suspected that Gus arranged his industrial crises in order to have more time to read. He had once developed a mysteriously painful back that was just as mysteriously cured when he had finished reading *War and Peace*.

When the money came, it was like an insurance policy being realised. All those times of worry when Gus had come home to say that was him finished with *that* job, all the nights lying in bed doing accounts in her head, a pound here and two pounds there, had eventually amounted to £3,500. She felt the justice of it. It didn't seem like an accident. It was the security she had surely earned. But it was only security as long as it was there. While it lay in the bank, she was safe from the daily irritations, the fraying of the nerves that thirty-five years of marriage to Gus had represented. He complained that she didn't use it. She was using it all the time. It lightened her housework. It sweetened every cup of coffee, sugared every doughnut. At

night she could bathe her mind in it like a Radox bath
before she went to sleep.

'What would be wrong wi' usin' some of it to go to
Canada? Ye won it at the football, anyway. Though how ye
did, Ah don't know. Ye wouldny know a right half from a
wee half.'

'No, you would, though. You would be drinkin' a lot of
wee halfs if you could get your hands on it.'

He was right about her knowing nothing about football
but that didn't diminish her belief in the justice of her win.
She had a dim image of a lot of young men running about
a lot of parks that fateful Saturday afternoon, doing the
strange things people do with a football, and she thought
there was a kind of fairness in the way they had conspired
to repay her for what she had suffered in the cause of the
game. For the importance of football to the Scots was yet
another of Gus's theories, one for which he seemed to feel
the need to do a lot of fieldwork. Every time Scotland and
England played at Hampden or Wembley, he was there, as
well as having been in Cardiff and Belfast. The way back
from such places always seemed to be fraught with hazard.
She was used to getting phone calls from Preston or Carlisle
or Dumfries two days after an international match had
finished to learn that a car had broken down without warning or a freak thunderstorm had flooded roads or one of the
men he was with had been taken to hospital with acute
something-or-other. Her exasperation had come to a climax
the last time he had done it. When he announced himself,
she had said, 'Gus who?' and put the phone down. When
he got home, she said she had thought it was one of those
funny phone calls.

'It wouldn't take that much,' Gus said.

'Listen! You want to go tae the Rockies. Go. Ye've got
ma blessing.' The film was obviously coming to an interesting part. 'Ah'll maybe get watchin' the television in peace.
But ye don't get a penny from me.'

'Ah would've done it for you.'

'The money's mine!'

'On the other side, it may be said that Avarice is the quintessence of all vices,' Schopenhauer said.

'You really want me to go?'

'Go.'

She knew she was safe enough. He had always been struggling to get as far as London for a game. It looked as if the train was heading for a terrible accident. It was a good thing they had Charlton Heston there.

'All right –'

'Sh!'

There was an ear-shattering crash. The train buckled and slewed terrifyingly. Carriages came off the rails, rolled over, burst open. More circus animals than you would have thought the train could hold broke free from the wreckage – elephants, lions, horses and others Jeanie wasn't sure she could identify – and ran in various directions over the countryside. Steam hissed from the broken engine. People were injured and bleeding. They found Charlton Heston almost crushed to death, a huge girder that nobody could move lying across his chest.

'The thing is, Jeanie –'

'Sh!'

The small sound was like a whiplash to Gus's dignity. He was trying to talk about something of major importance and his wife had no time for him. He felt as if he was being cuckolded by the television. Just on cue, like the other man entering at exactly the wrong moment, Charlton spoke.

'We may miss the matinée,' he said from under his girder, 'but we'll make the evening show.'

'Jesus Christ!' Gus was on his feet. 'How can you sit there an' watch that shite? Ah resent ma hoose gettin' used as a sewer for Hollywood. Look at that! Look at it!' He was over beside Jeanie, pointing towards the screen. 'He was lyin' under enough metal there tae rebuild the *Tirpitz*. There couldn't be a bone in his body that wasn't broken. There's wild animals miles away by this time. There must be folk all over the neighbourhood gettin' chewed alive and trampled to daith. Evenin' show? Who's gonny be the audience? How can you sit there an' watch that? An' that daft Cornel Wilde. He talks about women as if they were an off-licence. An' that Betty Hutton! Singin' and dancin' on a trampoline at the same time. Do you believe that tripe? See that Cecil B. De Mille. He must've had a heid like a corporation coup.'

Jeanie hadn't taken her eyes off the television.

'Ach, away an' get yer train through the Rockies,' she said.

'You've said it!' Gus was pointing at her, imposing as a figure in a Victorian print – The Outraged Husband. 'That's exactly where Ah'm goin'. And no comebacks from you. Don't start moanin' when Ah do. Because you think Ah can't do it. Without your money. You and yer money! The Bloody Heiress. Well, Ah'm goin', Missus. Just watch me go. Ah'm Rockies bound.'

'Cheerio,' Jeanie said.

Gus took Schopenhauer, who was still in his hand, and threw him viciously across the room. He grabbed his jacket from the back of a chair and put it on. He stood in the middle of the floor. He looked at Jeanie.

'The only way tae get your attention,' he said, 'is tae appear on the telly. As long as it's a bad programme. If it's no' shite, ye'll still no' be noticed. Missus, yer brains are mince. When Ah married you, Ah volunteered for a lobotomy.'

He went out. Jeanie tried to go on watching the television but the film had turned to farce before her eyes. She heard Gus's voice as a mocking commentary over it, as a mocking commentary over her life. She felt silly watching it. She felt silly being her.

She rose and crossed to the window. She watched him

reach the end of the street with his sailor's walk. 'On ye go,' she muttered. 'But ye'll not go far.'

She crossed to where the book lay. She picked it up and looked at the cover. The face on the front was that of a peppery old man with flyaway hair. He looked like a troublemaker. She sneered at the face. 'Worse than fancy women,' she muttered.

She went through to the kitchen and opened the bin. Taking out the plastic shopping-bag that was full of rubbish, she checked that it contained suitably messy materials. There were egg shells and greasy paper and pieces of fat and the remains of some custard. As she opened the book, she noticed places where Gus had underlined parts and marked them with a biro star. These were the places she was most careful to smear with custard and grease.

She pushed the book to the bottom of the rubbish and tied the handles of the shopping-bag in a knot. She went outside. Standing with the dustbin lid in her hand, she glanced up. The view was of dull back-gardens hemmed in by scabrously weathered council houses. It was the terminal vista of her life. But it would also be his. She painstakingly took out all the other plastic bags, put the one she had brought out at the bottom and covered it with the replaced bags. She put the lid back on the dustbin. 'We'll see what he does now,' she muttered.

She came back in and closed the door and started to wash her hands in preparation for making his supper, which she would leave out for him when she went to bed.

17

Hullo again

Recognition came to him between dessert and coffee. He had noticed her earlier, sitting opposite another woman and talking with a slightly actressy animation, given to *ingénue* gestures that belied her age, as if life hadn't discovered her yet. He had seen a woman in her forties with hair that still looked naturally dark, eyes that were still interested and a body that was nicely substantial. When he realised that he knew her, that he owned, as it were, a small part of her past, his glances had become less cursory, more proprietary. She's weathered well, he thought. I wonder.

Recognising her was a moment of small adventure for him, a pulse of adolescence in a middle-aged day. The pretentious restaurant, chosen by his client, briefly seemed a place where something might happen and the deadness of occasion animate to an event. Even the proprietor's manner seemed less obtrusive. He was a small, numbingly bright man who had fixed an expression of jollity to his face like a Hallowe'en mask. He mistook interference for attentiveness and flippancy for wit. His blandishments had threatened the meal, for eating in his presence was like having everything drenched in syrup.

He appeared to know the client well and perhaps they deserved each other. The client was a self-made man who had long ago ceased to notice that most of the parts were missing. 'What I always say is' was what he always said. He had started out 'as a silly boy with nothing' and after years of unremitting effort and deals of legendary deviousness had successfully transformed himself into a silly man with nothing, except an awful lot of money. He had spent most of the lunch expressing his modestly oblique astonishment at why other people couldn't be more like him. 'What I always say is whiners create their own difficulties.' If everybody would get out and do as he had done, they could be in the same position as he was. The thought of a nation of near-millionaires seemed to present him with no logistical problems. He disarmed any suggestion of egotism with frequent references to how much he owed to God. He referred to God as if He might be a senior partner with a particularly astute sense of the market.

'I did it,' he was saying. 'And what's so special about me?'

His audience smiled and said, 'Excuse me. I've just seen someone I know. Do you mind? Won't be a minute.'

He rose and walked towards her table. He saw her glance towards him and back to her companion. He enjoyed the stages of her recognition. The first look had simply been acknowledging someone moving in the restaurant. When she looked back, it was because she had belatedly registered that he was looking at her. She stared, wondering why he should be coming towards her table. The need to understand focused her attention and he saw her eyes widen in surprise as he walked out of strangeness into familiarity. Being recognised for who he had been stimulated his own sense of the past and he remembered her name just in time. She half-stood up in confusion.

'Eddie Cameron,' she said.

'Marion. You haven't changed a bit. I recognised you right away.'

He kissed her on the cheek and, as soon as he had done it, knew the action was a moment of inspiration, for the kiss was a cipher of past intimacy. It made them a conspiracy of two in the crowded room.

'I was amazed,' he said. 'There's Marion, I thought. I was going to come over earlier but you both seemed so engrossed.'

'Oh, this is Jane Thomas. Jane, Eddie Cameron.'

As he shook hands, he noticed that the woman, whose back had been towards him, was as plain as a loaf and he wondered again if pretty women sometimes chose their friends like accessories to highlight themselves. Marion had sat back down.

'It's Jane's birthday,' she said. 'We work in the same office. We're out celebrating.'

'If celebrating's the word,' Jane said.

'Anyway, congratulations or condolences, Jane. Choose your pick. You look good on it, anyway.'

'The wine,' Jane confided.

'You should keep taking the medicine then.'

'Thank you, doctor.'

He was glad that their brief coquetry caused Marion to butt in like someone at an excuse-me dance.

'What are you doing here?' she said.

'Business. It's been a long time since I was in this town. It's changed so much.'

'Not for the better,' Jane said.

'I'm lost in it now,' he said. 'What about you, Marion?' He glanced at her rings. 'Happily married with ten of a family?'

'I'm a widow.'

She didn't say it casually. Her voice went into mourning and he wondered how recently it had happened.

'God, I'm sorry, Marion,' he said and felt a quickening of interest. 'Obviously, I didn't know. That was clumsy.'

'You weren't to know. It's been seven years now.'

The information made the tone in which she had declared her widowhood seem a bit extravagant. He was reminded of a woman he knew who was inclined to intone every so often, 'Father would have been ninety-five by now.' Or ninety-six. Or, the following year unsurprisingly, ninety-seven. It had led to a joke with his wife. 'Father would have been a hundred and forty-two by now. Pity he died at nineteen.'

'Any children?' he asked casually.

'Two,' Marion said soulfully, as if the shadow of dark wings had fallen across the cheese-board. Inexplicably, he felt the prospect of the evening brighten.

'That's good,' he said. 'Best invention in the world, children.'

He sensed Jane's face opening towards him like a flower.

'I know what you mean,' she said. 'They can be a trial. But they're what it's all about as far as I'm concerned. Mine are taking me out tonight. I'd better sober up before then. They're choosing the restaurant. Wait till you see. John, he's the oldest. He's been taking charge of all arrangements. Won't let Michael – that's my husband – even know where we're going. And Darren, the youngest, he's been threatened within an inch of his life if he reveals the dreaded secret. He's been bursting to tell me all week.'

'Lucky you,' Eddie said, hoping to forestall the taking of snapshots from her handbag. 'I'll probably go and read the cemetery. Catch up on news of old friends.' The gaffe of being flippant about death so soon after Marion's mention of her dead husband made him move on quickly. 'And what about you, Marion? What wild plans have you got for tonight?'

Marion's close-lipped smile was wan as a fading rose in memory of her husband.

'She doesn't go out nearly enough,' Jane said. 'I've been telling her that.'

'So you should,' Eddie prompted.

'An attractive woman like her.'

'A *very* attractive woman like her.'

Their pincer movement was neatly trapping Marion in their sense of her. She seemed to be enjoying the mild embarrassment.

'It's such a waste,' Jane said.

'You get out of the way of going out.' Marion was on the defensive. 'Mixing with people.'

'I know what you mean,' Eddie said.

'It's no excuse,' Jane said.

'Here!' Eddie said, as if it was something that had only just come into his mind. 'What about dinner with me tonight, Marion? You'd be doing me a favour. It's either that or counting the perforations in the tea-bag in my hotel room.'

'Eddie!'

'Why not?'

'Why not, Marion?' Jane said.

'For old times' sake,' Eddie said. 'An innocent meal between old friends. A good way for you to break the ice again. No complications.'

'I don't think I could take another bite after this,' Marion said.

'Then we'll eat the ambience. What you say?'

'She says yes.'

'Jane!'

'Well, you do.'

'I don't know. What about Michael and Lucy?'

'Look. You two going back to your office now?'

Jane nodded.

'Okay. You think about it, Marion. If you give me the office number, I'll phone you there this afternoon. It's all right. If it's no, I promise not to take an overdose.' Jane had already taken a pen from her handbag and she wrote the number on the flap of an envelope, tore it off and handed it to Eddie.

'Sweet lady,' he said. 'A birthday beverage for you. What's it to be?'

'Oh, I've had enough. I'll be singing at the switchboard.'

'Please. Let me make the gesture. People should sing on their birthday. Maybe a sad song. But they should sing. A liqueur. What's your favourite liqueur?'

'She likes Tia Maria,' Marion said.

'What about you, Marion?'

Marion was hesitant, as if saying yes once might develop into a habit.

'I don't know that I should.'

'I'm not drinking on my own,' Jane said.

'Green Chartreuse then.'

Even egregious sycophancy has its uses. The proprietor's overeagerness meant that Eddie's gesture was interpreted as it happened. He was grateful, for he could remember other occasions when he had thought he would have to let off a flare to get a waiter. This time the moment came clean out of the films of his boyhood. The small ceremony complete, he asked the proprietor to add the drinks to his bill.

'Happy birthday, Jane,' he said. 'Nice to have met you. Marion. You'll hear me calling you.'

They were laughing as he left. The client wasn't. His conversation was a lecture. He didn't like it when the audience walked out. Eddie offered more coffee like paying a fine and put on his listening expression while his thoughts went off on their own.

The piece of paper in his pocket interested him: the first number in the combination to a safe. What would be inside? He looked back at Marion and she sketched a toasting gesture with her glass. She smiled and he smiled back, exchanging sealed communications – billets doux or blank paper? It occurred to him that neither knew what the other meant. It occurred to him that they didn't know yet what they meant themselves.

The room pleased him now. It had lost its predetermined crassness, sanctified for him by his renewal of the sense of mystery. Its garish brightness had become luminous and, hearing the faint clash of cutlery and the voices baffled into an indecipherable human murmur by his mood, he felt the happy strangeness of being there.

He watched Marion and her friend rise and begin those female preparations for leaving that he loved, the retrieving of scarves and umbrellas, the finding of handbags, the gathering of coats – not so much a leaving as a flitting. It was as if they briefly set up house wherever they went. As they were walking out, they waved. He waved to Jane. Towards Marion he pointed his right hand like a gun, winked along his forefinger and clicked down his thumb.

'How do you know her?' the client asked.

As the wine wore off during the afternoon, Jane grew doubtful about her part in getting Eddie to phone the office. She had a determinedly married woman's superstition about the things that might threaten the comfortable stability of her marriage. It was a kind of psychological housewifery: leave crumbs and you get mice. What irritated her late in the afternoon was that she had left crumbs.

Her attitudes were usually well dusted and neatly in place. The overall structure that housed them was simple but substantial: marriage is too important to play around with. Inside that monumental certainty all her responses fitted comfortably. Whatever situation cropped up, she knew where it went. If a man tried to chat you up, you didn't allow it. You didn't involve yourself with married friends who were interested in other men. If you got out of work early, you did shopping or came home.

Coming back from the restaurant in the taxi they had to take because they were late, Marion had said, 'But he's married!'

'How do you know? He doesn't wear a ring.'

'He must be married. And he mentioned children.'

'Maybe he's divorced.'

'He would have said.'

'We didn't ask him. Or maybe he'll get divorced after tonight.'

The glibness of the remark turned acid in her conscience. How could she have said that? She felt she had betrayed some unknown woman. She felt she had betrayed Michael and the children. She believed that to be dismissive about other people's marriages was somehow to tempt providence in relation to your own. She shouldn't have taken so much wine, she thought. When she was relieved at the switchboard to get her coffee, she was still troubled.

'That Eddie Cameron,' she said to Marion. 'How do you know him?'

'We used to know each other years ago. When we were still in our teens.'

'First love,' Jane's love of categories suggested.

'First something.'

'And you haven't seen him since?'

'More than twenty years. I don't know how he recognised me.'

'You made up your mind yet?'

'I thought I might leave that to you. You seem to have decided everything else for me.'

'No complications, he said.'

Jane said it to herself as much as to Marion and she took the thought away with her like a plea for the defence. She had acted in all innocence, she told herself. But she couldn't avoid the thought that she wouldn't like Michael to behave like Eddie Cameron. She couldn't believe that he would, for very practical reasons. Their marriage was a highly efficient radar system by which each could plot the exact position of the other at any given time of day or night. There wouldn't have been room for another woman in Michael's life unless he was secretly making one out of hardboard in his workroom or growing her from a seed in the greenhouse.

Hearing Eddie Cameron's voice on the phone and putting

him through to Marion, Jane felt herself an accomplice in a crime. At the end of the day, as they both collected their coats, Jane asked Marion a question with her eyes and Marion nodded.

'Michael and Lucy are going to my sister's,' she said.

Jane hurried home to hold on to her domesticity like a talisman.

During dinner they tried to find out who each other was. Her married name was Bland and when she mentioned 'Harry' (which she did often enough for the word to be a conjunction, about as essential to her expression of herself as 'and'), Eddie suspected that he had known her late husband. He didn't mention the fact. If he was right, his sense of Harry Bland hardly squared with Marion's hushed reverence. Entering the sanctum with hob-nailed boots was no part of seduction.

'He was a salesman, too, you know,' Marion said.

'Hm,' Eddie said.

She mentioned Jane Thomas's worries about what Marion might be getting herself into and waited. He dutifully explained about his separation and divorce, and how often he saw his daughters. He told her about the time he had worked in the bookshop and noticed her soften slightly, confronted with a man of some sensitivity, who had concerns beyond the material.

As the evening progressed, he noted a certain morbid tendency in her to refer to death. He forestalled it with levity. It was as if Harry's death had given her a Ph.D. in the subject. Once she mentioned the beatific expression on Harry's face as he stared towards the ceiling before he died. 'He was probably thinking he'd never have to paint another cornice,' Eddie said to himself but not to her.

'Have you ever watched anyone dying, Eddie?' she said.

'I suppose I have.'

'Have you really?'

'You sound surprised.'

'I wouldn't have guessed somehow.'

'What it is,' he said, 'I'm not wearing my death-watcher's badge tonight.'

Shared moments from the past made up much of the talk. They sat like lepidopterists comparing specimens. It was encouraging how well their memories matched. It was only occasionally that he had a Red Admiral and she had a moth. By the second bottle of wine, those fragile butterflies seemed to be shaking themselves free of their pins and fluttering in the room around them, there to be caught all over again. The air seemed full of possibilities.

'Eddie,' she said. 'You know that I can't take you home with me. It's been too long. I just can't.'

'Of course not,' he said. 'I understand.'

At her place they drank coffee. While their mouths discussed how soon he would have to leave, the physical sensations they had generated in each other circled their conversation like patient muggers, waiting for their moment. He precipitated the moment by getting up to leave. He crossed to the door.

'Eddie,' she said. 'Put out the light.'

He didn't question her. He put out the light. He stood in the darkness, listening to the sounds of her undressing beside the couch where he had left her. As if hypnotised by those sweet, furtive whisperings of cloth, he began to do the same. He started to feel his way towards her.

'Please don't be rough, Eddie,' she said.

'Darlin', I may never find you,' he said.

But he did and, by the unromantic light of an electric fire, her with one of her suspenders flapping loose, him with his socks still on, they made that mysterious and awesome transition from having sex to making love. Their bodies led them out past attitudes to wander looking for each other in an authentic darkness lust had made. His clever mouth went infant. Seduction was a second language he had never effectively learned and he reverted to honest, desperate babbling and ate her as the uttermost expression of his meaning. In the heat Harry was incinerated. The past was cast like clothes and she became sheer, voracious present. They forged their bodies into weird shapes and cooled into strangers, not to each other, to themselves.

It was strange to sit holding each other and, watching the fire, wonder who you were.

Bed seemed a kind of solution. They talked gentle irrelevancies to each other and kissed and tried to sleep. But they couldn't sleep. How do you sleep when you're lying in a stranger's body? They got out of bed and tried to find roles to play.

Marion made more coffee. Eddie suggested fixing a screw to the handle of the door but Marion didn't know where there was a screwdriver. The jokes this led to between them were a relief. Finding themselves laughing, they both began to use jokes as a discreet conspiracy, dead leaves with which to smother the awkwardly living thing they had made between them.

Marion found an old photograph of them with Eddie striking a rather dramatic pose. They remembered the wincing pretentiousness of his teens. Marion went in search of a phrase he had been fond of using that would illustrate exactly how pretentious he had been. Eddie was trying to help her.

'I've got it, I've got it,' she said.

'Good,' Eddie said unconvincingly.

'You said,' she said. 'You said – wait for this. You were going to live life . . . It wasn't to the hilt. That's not what you said. Curmudgeon or something. Dudgeon. That was it. You were going to live life to the dudgeon. You said that. Whatever the hell it means.'

'It means the same as hilt,' Eddie said. 'I think I was trying to show I'd read *Macbeth* at school. "And on the blade and dudgeon gouts of blood." Jesus, that's embarrassing.'

'Live life to the dudgeon. How about that? That's what you should call your memoirs. "How High Was My Dudgeon"!'

Eddie thought she was going to wet herself. He laughed loudly and waited. As they talked on, trying to exorcise the hours of darkness until normalcy could resume, both sensed how frenetic the conversation was becoming and how much closer to cruelty it was moving. But perhaps because of the guilt of what they were deliberately, if discreetly, doing or perhaps because daylight was coming near and there were still disturbing signs of life under the dead leaves, they made no attempt to stop themselves. They orchestrated a quarrel. It was as if they had tacitly agreed, 'If the bloody thing won't lie still, let's use shovels.'

Harry provided the soil. Marion had found some photographs of him. She didn't just show them to Eddie. She kept setting them in gilt-frames of anecdote, touching them up into icons. She was re-instating Harry in his shrine and doing penance before it for her unworthiness, as exemplified, presumably, by what they had done tonight.

'Selective embalming,' Eddie said.

Marion's smile became a wound.

'Why do you say that? You don't know what a good person he was.'

'If that's what bothers you, you can forget it. Because I knew him.'

'You're lying. How could you be so sure?'

'Harry Bland. Worked for Maynard's, didn't he? I thought I knew the name. And the photos clinched it.'

'You're lying. You would've said before this.'

'I don't like desecrating shrines.'

'You seem to manage.'

'I didn't know then that the deity was malign.'

'Oh, you're lying.'

'Maynard's. Area Supervisor. Right? I met him more

than once. Conferences. Once in London with people I knew. Not official biographer status, right enough. But enough to get a perspective. I always remember he had the top of a finger missing. How's that for a birthmark?'

'That's right.'

Marion gathered all the photographs and replaced them in the shoe-box. She put the lid on very carefully, nursing the box on her lap.

'If you knew him at all,' she said, 'then you'll understand how lousy I feel in comparison.'

'No.'

'Then you didn't know him.'

'I know that he chased tail. With what amounted to dedication. Not too successfully but keenly.'

'Get to hell out of my flat!'

'I'm not dressed for a dramatic exit.'

'Just leave! Get out!'

'Oh, piss off,' he said. 'You're like a sparrow thinks its being victimised by winter. Nobody's after you. It's just if you talk you're liable to bump into the truth now and again. You better stop letting your thoughts run around in sentences. They'll get knocked down. And if you insist on clinching with people, naturally you'll burst your oxygen tent. And you'll have to breathe real air.'

'What you're saying isn't the truth.'

'Of course, it is.'

'How do you know?'

'Because I heard people who knew him well say it. Without malice. And I saw him trying to operate a couple of times.'

'With women?'

'It was all boringly heterosexual.'

'You're a bastard!'

'Accolades, accolades.'

'I don't believe you.'

'Then don't.'

They went on and Marion painstakingly outlined to Eddie just what an utterly pathetic object he was. He was, it seemed, a superannuated philanderer, a case of severely arrested development and someone who had – triumphant moment of finding the killing phrase – 'acne of the eyes'. He infected whatever he looked at with his own disease.

Eddie constructed a rococo verbal edifice in his defence. The way he lived was, apparently, the nature of the game. You had to lose a lot of conventional attitudes trying to find that occasional chord which put the jangle of coincidence in tune. Private lives were getting slightly passé, anyway. They had the television for a mirror. Pretty soon they would all be able to copulate by post. It was old-fashioned of him to want to confront his privacy in a full-length, wasting mirror every so often. He made himself sound slightly heroic.

They went on, she in her dressing-gown and slippers, he in trousers and bare feet with his jacket over his naked body, his paunch protruding coyly. Coffee dregs congealed and were thawed out with fresh brewings. The cigarette-stubs sank in a sea of ash.

Among the sound of the first starlings, she said, 'I believe you.'

'Sorry?'

'I believe you.'

'How do you mean?'

'About Harry. Damn you!'

'As long as you don't damn him. He didn't ask to be canonised.'

'I feel like not bothering to go on.'

'No you don't. You've only lost something you never had. Nothing to be done about that.'

When it was fully light, he brought in the milk and made more coffee and toast. They breakfasted in silence. He dressed and came over to her. She stood up. They embraced and felt the earth move – not the world, just the rubbish they had heaped on that moment of disturbing love they had experienced together. The feeling was still alive. They looked at each other.

'Are you going to phone?' she asked.

He winked.

'Maybe from Mars.'

She smiled.

'I'll be out.'

He went back to the hotel and showered and shaved and put on fresh clothes. He saw two clients in the morning but his conversations with them were like transatlantic telephone calls. He was aware of a recurring gap between what they said and his assimilation of it. His eyes were sparking. He began to think that, functioning like this, he should be on commission from a rival firm.

He was back in the hotel by 12.30. He lunched in a dining-room where two women whispered among the empty tables and through the window two old men played the nine-hole putting-green in anoraks. The way their caps, unresisted by any hair, fitted themselves to their heads saddened him. They tottered about the grass like a vision of the future. He saw his life relentless as a corridor. From now on there wouldn't be many doors that opened off it.

Upstairs, he stripped to shirt, trousers and socks and lay on the bed. He didn't sleep. He regretted telling her about Harry. He didn't regret telling her about Harry. He regretted the way he had told her about Harry. He could be a cruel bastard.

He remembered Allison, his ex-wife – whom God preserve, but far from him – engaging in one of her scenes from the Theatre of the Absurd, during one of those dramatic quarrels that made Eugene O'Neill seem laconic. She had emerged from the bathroom to announce grandly that she had been trying to slit her wrists. He had made the mistake of rushing towards her to comfort her. A magnifying glass could have detected a red line across each wrist. His anger at himself for falling for yet another of her fakeries had made him bitter.

'You won't win any death-certificates with that,' he had said.

'You'd think it was funny if I *was* dying,' she had said.

'Considering the rate at which you're losing blood, you can't have more than twenty years. With a tourniquet you might stretch that to thirty. You should get an elastoplast. It's not very dramatic to die of septic wrists.'

He didn't like himself for having said that. He didn't like what he'd become. How long was it since he had thought of Margaret Sutton, who had loved him and who had killed herself? He was the one who as a teenager couldn't watch anybody cry without finding tears in his own eyes. He felt some of that softness re-activate as he thought of Marion. He wanted to protect her. Perhaps he wanted her to protect him, too. He wanted his head examined.

He thought of a joke card he had bought and put in the alcove in the sitting-room of his flat. It showed a tall, bare-breasted woman standing in the middle of a maze. A small, down-trodden man was standing outside the maze, looking at her and saying, 'The last time I went into one of those it took me five years to get out.' The small man had been lucky.

My life is orderly, he told himself. So is a headstone, he told himself. You want to play that game again? he asked himself. You know another one that matters? he asked himself. At the moment Marion and he were two separate, contained confusions. Together, they could grow into a disaster. Neither of them needed that. But, beyond rationality, small images were budding in his memory, irrelevant as flowers. The softness of her upper arms. The way her head had found his neck before they parted.

He got up and walked about the room. 'No way,' he said aloud. But it was years since he had felt so alive. He became idiot with anonymity in the hotel room. He whistled and danced to himself in the mirror. He made pum-pum noises and snapped his fingers as he crossed the floor. He lay flat on the bed, reading the 'For Your Information' leaflet. Then he laid it on his face and carefully tested how hard he had to blow to blow it off. He noticed how squat his feet were in his socks. He found one tendril of dark cobweb dangling from the ceiling and for minutes watched it wafting gently.

'Chambermaid,' he said loudly. 'If your proficiency doesn't improve, you will be beaten to death with a feather-duster.' He laughed like the villain in a bad film.

He got up and crossed to the phone and dialled. He hoped she would speak to him. Jane Thomas's voice answered and, when he introduced himself, she was effusive in her welcome. It was presumably relief because Marion had explained that he wasn't married with fourteen of a family. The omens were propitious.

'Hullo,' Marion said.

'Hullo again,' he said and was talking not just to her but to what was left of the young man he had been.

18

Holing out

It was from the start a day of mild but persistent unease, nothing Bert Watson could pinpoint – a seediness in things, a kind of emotional dyspepsia. His favourite yellow golfing sweater was in the wash. The fat on the breakfast bacon wasn't crisp. It curled away like rubber when he knifed it to the edge of his plate. Robert was already playing records in his room. It sounded as if it was the same record all the time, something with an amazingly repetitive, thudding beat, like a musical headache. Marie sat across the table from him still in her dressing-gown, reading the paper and saying 'Ho!' every so often. He was careful not to ask for elucidation.

But these petty irritations weren't really what the feeling was about. They simply allowed him to realise that the feeling was there, moving sluggishly but inexorably inside him. They were like the rash that denotes an allergy. It felt as if it was an allergy to his own life.

He didn't like this house, had never really liked it. It had been a bargain at the time. Everybody said so. But what you didn't like couldn't be a bargain. Looking through the window, he could see the path in the garden he had often walked back and forth on – dimensions of his cell, bridge of his compassless ship.

He had wanted to write poetry. It seemed ridiculous at the moment. He was wearing a blue sweater and unhappy

with his bacon. He felt his life was an accident that had
happened to someone else. How could he ever have written
poetry? He was the manager of a hosiery.

But he suddenly remembered the experience of trying to
write. There had been one about the idea of sainthood, a
condemnation of it. All he could remember was the last line:
'They're welcome to their obscene innocence.' He must have
that poem somewhere. Lately, he had been dreaming of
writing the one poem that would express his life. A
dilettante's dream, he thought.

'Robert and Jennifer are both going to enter that essay
competition.' Marie said from behind her paper.

'Scribbling rivalry,' he said.

Marie didn't respond. He wondered when and why he
had developed his tendency to make puns. Perhaps it was
an attempt to subvert the banality of his life, suggest a
fifth-column of alternative meaning behind the ordinariness.
Perhaps that was why he had wanted to write poetry. He
tried to remember other poems he had written but they all
seemed so long ago, mental fossils in a folder somewhere in
some drawer, and Walter tooted the horn outside, making
his tired thoughts not so much scatter as hop indifferently
out of range.

Marie took his kiss like a corpse and the cheerio he
shouted upstairs bounced back off a wall of music. Sunlight
from the windscreen of Walter's car dazzled him so that he
stood on the path a moment in a spiral of darkness that
slowly led him back out to the light. In the car he felt
sustained by Walter's identity. There was the cigar-smoke
and Walter's voice like seamless piped music filling the car.
They would do it to them today and Maureen seemed to
have four periods a month these days and who was that daft
bastard in the Range Rover.

Tom and Frank were waiting for them in the locker-room.
While he changed slowly, pausing to pick some of the
hardened dirt from the spikes of his golf-shoes, Walter and

Tom talked business. He wondered whose business it was. It wasn't his. They made jokes that he seemed to miss for they teased him about it, sympathising with Walter about having to partner him. When they clattered out for some putting practice, he sat a little longer in the locker-room. He felt tired. Irrelevantly, he felt envious that Frank was taking a course at the Open University.

He played quite well. They halved the first two holes and Walter lost them the third by missing a two-foot putt. 'No gimmes,' Frank had said. At the fourth hole with Walter out of it, he chipped out of a bunker and holed out. They were all square. They called him Trevino for a couple of minutes.

But the sky seemed somehow too big for him. Walking down the fairways, he felt himself dwindling. He felt exposed. He wondered what he was doing here. The game appeared a strange convention he had never understood. His drive off the fifth tee was long but sliced into the rough. A five iron took him close to the hole but still in the rough. Helping him to find the ball, Walter said, 'You've got a good lie anyway'.

For no reason he could understand, he thought of two people. He thought of Duncan MacFarlane, who had gone to Argentina five years ago in 1978 and had returned and looked after his mother until she died, and then had gone to America. He thought of a boy called Sammy Nelson who had applied for a job and had been so ridiculously bright that it would have been an embarrassment to offer him such menial work. It's wrong, he thought. The whole thing's wrong. We're doing it wrong. The thought came to him simple and sheer, like an undeniable revelation. He held the vision of those two intense and honest and just faces in his mind and saw the enormity of the injustices ranged against them. He moved one hand helplessly in front of him, as if to bless them wherever they might be.

'What's the problem?' Walter shouted.

He decided on an eight iron. As he stood beside the ball taking practice swings, he was feeling strange. The rhythm of his swing had a life of its own. There was a core of dark in the light of the day. He wanted to shout but it wasn't what you did. In that moment he came to his double senses. All life was a game and you played by the rules, fair ways and foul, and your arms were just members of a club that they had joined. You stayed true to the lies where you found yourself, took the rough with the smooth, didn't care a pin. But he seemed to happen in a strange slow motion, held the top of the arc for a second too long, felt his stance was wrong and a lack of balance as the blue of the sky broke his concentration, understood this wasn't just a practice shot but a chip off the block of the one real thing. The ball he addressed was addressed to him – too late now to change direction. The bag was mixed and the game was rigged, the last hole what they put you in. But even as his heart – too early – broke, he followed through to the end, took one last stroke.

19

Deathwatch beetle

Morrison woke, suddenly staring into the darkness as if it was the barrel of a gun. Since he had come to prison two months ago, he slept like a hen. He was awake and he was terrified. He was awake because there was a noise in the cell. He was terrified because he didn't understand what the sound was. As he slowly deciphered the sound from the dark, he became much more terrified.

Rafferty was exercising. Morrison lay in the darkness listening. He didn't know what time it was but he estimated it to be the early hours of the morning. He was afraid to let it be known he was awake. He heard the steady, self-absorbed rhythm of Rafferty's breathing undermining the stillness of the night. Like a deathwatch beetle, he thought. It was the relentless patience of it that was so frightening. It knew no purpose but itself. It was a compelled progress nothing could deflect. The breathing communicated confidentially with the darkness, a mad language no one else could understand. But Morrison, enforced student of Rafferty as he was, was making his hesitant translation.

'I'm not stepping out of anybody's way ever again,' Rafferty had said. 'As long as I live. It's down to iron rations here. You find out who you are. That's who I am. Some men get sentimental about the outside. Cling to it like a belief in the afterlife. I don't do that. This is it. I wouldn't let a wasp sting me without getting the bastard.'

I'm a thief, Morrison repeated to himself like a prayer. I'm just a thief. I've never hurt anybody in my life. What am I doing among men like these? And Rafferty's breathing surrounded him, achieved articulation in his mind like a response.

'The nick's not a suspension of life,' Rafferty had said. 'It's a logical extension of it. The way the sewers are with plumbing. And the only way out is through. You have to find your own way through. I hate the way some people talk about the nick. You know? Like, paying your debt to society. Most of society've got no idea what they're charging you. They think they're removing you from society? They're shoving you right up its arse. They're showing you what society's really like. Because the nick's not a removal from society. It *is* society. Without the etiquette.'

I can't survive this, Morrison thought.

'There's men in here who breathe violently,' Rafferty said. 'They were probably putting the head on their mother's womb. They look at a cutlery drawer and see an armoury. Take it easy, people say. Avoid trouble. Keep a low profile. There's no low profiles in here. There's people in here catch the sound of a pimple bursting. They can smell your fear before you know it's there. So don't let it be there.'

It is, Morrison thought, it is.

'It's what you come out *as* that counts,' Rafferty said. 'Men get raped in here. You know the one they call Rhoda? Queer as a three-legged budgie. They use him like a roller-towel. Me, I want to be so honed. Anybody tries to take me, be like grabbing an open razor.'

Morrison remembered Rafferty today in the visiting room. The woman who must be his wife had been crying. Rafferty had sat for more than twenty minutes without moving. Everybody had started to notice. Rafferty had a silence that could fill a room. In their cell Rafferty had said simply, 'She's leaving me.' Morrison had muttered something about maybe she wouldn't.

'It's all in the black box,' Rafferty said.

It was only now, his mind sharpened by fear, that Morrison understood what he meant. The black box was the part that survived the aircraft crash intact. It was the machine that went to the extremities of experience and came back with the answer to what had happened. On the basis of its findings, understanding could be achieved and blame apportioned. And action taken.

Morrison panicked. The sound of Rafferty's breathing was looking for someone, burrowing unstoppably towards a destination. Would it be him? He felt the injustice of his position, as he felt the injustice of Rafferty's. Why was it like this? He wanted to scream. He sensed the sound of Rafferty's breathing pushing out endlessly into the night. Then Rafferty stopped. There was a shuffling noise. Morrison knew that he had started doing press-ups. He was counting. 'One . . . two . . . three . . . four . . . five . . . six . . .' His voice was quiet.

Morrison in his dread imagined the count being taken up all over the country by men in dark places that weren't as dark as their hearts, the legions of the dispossessed, the terminally disenchanted, the keepers of accounts their society refused to honour.

'Twenty-two . . . twenty-three . . . twenty-four . . . twenty-five . . .'

I hope they get you, Morrison was saying to himself like a placative prayer that would fend off Rafferty. I hope they get you. I didn't cause this mess. I'm just a thief, an incompetent thief. It's you they're after, you in your big houses and your fancy cars, the ones who've forgotten to care, the ones who think that poverty is a personal choice and that exploitation is a birthright and that pain is a weakness. It's you they're after. He bit his finger to stop from shouting and cringed from Rafferty's voice which sounded to him like some strange talking calendar or the countdown to some terrible event.

'Eighty-five,' Rafferty said. 'Eighty-six . . . eighty-seven . . . eighty-eight . . . eighty-nine . . .'

20

Dreaming

H e was dreaming.
    'Sammy! Sammy!'
  He woke to the awareness first of the comfort of his room, the protective stacks of paperback books and the colourful posters on the wall and then, beyond the window, the sky looking as if it had been quarried from grey slate. He wasn't who he had been dreaming he was. He was Sammy Nelson.
  'Sammy!'
  'Okay.'
  'Time you were up. You've got that interview.'
  'What time is it? That's in the afternoon.'
  'Doesn't matter. It's the early bird that catches the worm.'
  'Don't like worms.'
  And then his father's voice: 'That's enough o' that. You're not too big to hit.'
  'Ladies and gentlemen, it's the Cliché Show. As you know the object of the game is to talk for as long as possible without saying anything of your own. Today's contestants: Peter and Mary Nelson, who have been practising for years. And remember, if you make the mistake of uttering one original thought or using a form of words that you didn't read somewhere or get from someone else, you will hear this sound . . . And disqualification will be immediate.'
  Playing with the idea outwitted the boringness of washing and getting dressed. He had wondered about shaving. But

he couldn't be bothered going on safari across his face to find the isolated prickles that were hiding out there. You had to turn your head all different ways to flush the fair hairs out into the light. He thought perhaps he should be more hairy at seventeen. But the problem was rendered irrelevant by the faces he made at himself in the mirror. He mugged himself into a kind of maturity that he brought downstairs with him

'Aye, maw. Da.'

'Mornin', son,' his mother said. 'My, you look smart.'

'Not before time,' his father said.

Sammy liked his parents. He had begun to realise how kind his mother was and his father's grumpiness was not offensive so much as defensive, like a dog barking because it's frightened you might come too close to it. But he was aware of the bafflement with which they regarded him. He felt it in the room now.

With his mother, it was a kind of head-shaking incomprehension, as if she would be forever trying to work out what he meant. His awareness of the feeling had repeatedly crystallised itself on the occasions that he brought his report cards home from school. He remembered the awe with which his mother had once mouthed to herself the word 'precocious'. Perhaps he had been, he thought dispassionately. He had certainly never found schoolwork any trouble.

With his father, it was a deep suspiciousness. His father couldn't understand how a son of his could have earned entrance to university. And then he couldn't understand why he hadn't taken it up. Sammy wasn't sure he understood either and he wasn't sure he cared. But he often caught his father looking at him oddly, perhaps wondering if he was a changeling.

His father was looking at him that way now, as Sammy ate his breakfast. His father was developing one of his favourite conversational themes, assisted by his mother. It was the 'What kind of son have we reared?' theme. It was a stylised performance in which the person under discussion was frequently referred to in the third person, as if he weren't present.

'Ah mean, can ye believe it?' his father was saying. 'Spending the day just readin' books? And playin' records. It's not natural.'

'Your father's right,' his mother was saying.

'It's not natural.'

'You should get more fresh air. A boy your age.'

'When Ah was his age, Ah was bringin' in a wage.'

'He does bring money into the house, Peter. Give him that.'

'And where does he get it? And television, that's another thing. If he's not readin' books, he's watchin' telly. Every thing and anything. Opera!'

'You do watch too much telly, son.'

'He watches bloody opera.'

Sammy realised it was less a conversation than a duet. He smiled affectionately to himself and looked at his parents. His mother, at the sink with the frying-pan in her hands covered with suds, was wearing Victorian mourning. His father was a caricature working-man, collarless shirt, sleeves rolled up. His face had haggard lines from make-up. The music was allegro.

'Whence comes this child?' his father's tenor voice sang.

'Wanton and wild,' his mother's soprano answered.

'Nay, we know not –' their voices blending.

'Is he our own?'

'Or made of stone?'

'Nay, we know not.'

'When will this end?'

'When we're round the bend?'

'Nay, we know not.'

There was more. Sammy enjoyed it fine. He rinsed his plate, knife and fork and coffee-mug under the hot water tap before putting them in the basin to be washed. His mother smiled to herself. She was a believer in small omens. She knew that as long as he kept the natural considerateness for others he seemed always to have shown, there was still hope for him.

The morning passed pleasantly enough. Sammy was given temporary absolution from learning the catechism of his inadequacies. His mother was busy in the house. His father was pottering out the back. He was on his two nights off, starting today, and that part of the week always quietened slightly the perpetual grumbling of his nature, like a dog that forgets what it was barking about and becomes interested in smells again. Tonight he would have a few beers and that might help.

Sammy read the paper, amazed all over again at the lives of other people. There was a story about a man dying of asbestosis, who was having difficulty claiming compensation. The asbestos factory where he had worked was implying that he hadn't always taken as many precautions as he should have. The point seemed ludicrous to Sammy. He was a man and he had worked for them most of his life and now he was dying because of it. Sammy felt that the man's very life had in a way been manufactured into the objects of which the asbestos was a part, and now the remains of it were being discarded like industrial waste.

Sammy read a little from three of the books he was involved with at the moment. But nothing seized him. He put on television and watched a programme for children under school-age. The elaborate behaviour of the presenters fascinated him. They made a conspiratorial mystery of trivia. They mimed everything they were saying. Sammy wondered why childhood should be treated like idiocy. Still, he didn't suppose it would do the children any harm. It might permanently damage the presenters, though. He imagined them in the pub after a day's work, walking like great big giants towards the bar, miming what they wanted to drink and rolling their eyes in astonished pleasure when they tasted it. He tried out the technique briefly at the lunch table.

'Ah told ye,' his father said. 'He's bloody daft.'

'No, Ah was watchin' Play School there,' Sammy said. 'It gets to you after a while.'

'Bloody Play School,' his father said. 'And he's supposed to be applyin' for a job.'

'Don't do that during yer interview, anyway,' his mother said.

The interview was a nonsense, as Sammy had suspected it would be. The job was for a junior clerk in a local government office. There were over two hundred applicants for the post. Sammy was, the man decided immediately, over-qualified. But that didn't terminate the interview.

The man wanted to tell him things, deep things, things that might change his life, it seemed. He was a heavy-set man who said 'Good Morning' as if it was a comment you might want to make a note of.

'I'd like to help you,' the man was still saying after more than five minutes. 'So few of you youngsters today understand what life is really about. You're going to have to learn. That's the real world out there.'

The man gazed mystically out of the window. What was out there was a brown-brick shopping precinct that was looking tatty by the time they finished putting it up, some houses, factories, most of them closed or closing. But it could have been the roof of the world and the man was interpreting the whole of life for Sammy like a map. The man turned back towards Sammy. He looked at him with kind condescension. It was obviously a key moment. The air in the room tensed in preparation for the weight of the pronouncement it would have to take.

'Work,' the man said. He didn't say where you were to find it. 'Work.' He waited. Big meanings take a long time to absorb. 'Effort. Sheer effort.' He looked as if running for a bus would give him a cardiac arrest. 'Effort. And then again effort. Work. You get nothing for nothing.'

Sammy's eyes were going out of focus trying to concentrate on the unreality of what was going on. This man was talking garbage in a holy voice. One of his father's favourite words for Sammy, always offered as an accusation, was 'dreamer'. But who was dreaming here? Did this man really believe the platitudes he was intoning? He certainly seemed to. Sammy could almost smell the incense. He felt the room go dim as a Buddhist temple. Somewhere candles were burning.

'I'll give you this,' the man was saying.

It was a general application form for employment in local government, one for the files. It was the third time the man had offered it to him. Each time he had withdrawn it again, perhaps feeling that he hadn't yet sufficiently impressed on Sammy the sacredness of the document.

'I'll give you this. Now don't lose it. Don't forget about it. Fill it in. Use it. Return it to us. Who knows . . .'

Sammy stared at the man in disbelief. He was the eastern guru in the Guinness advertisement Sammy had seen on television, imparting the secrets of the universe to his bald-headed novitiate, Grasshopper. His saffron robe glowed in the dingy office. Behind his wispy moustache and beard, his lips moved with the wisdom of the ages.

'Glasshoppah. There many thing in life we cannaw understan. Why ver, very, rish people sit on fat arses for forty year and just get risher. Ah, why, Glasshoppah? Is ordained. Poor people must stay poor, Glasshoppah. And must be happy as a pig in shit. Look. I give you this. Paypah? Piece of paypah? Glasshoppah, you have mush to learn. Is secret of universe. You make necessary maks on this piece paypah. All thing come to pass. You get job. Job, Glasshoppah. Shitty job, but job. You work forty, fifty year. Your blain turn to cement. Happiness. Happiness, Glasshoppah, is not being able to think. We teach you how.

Take magic paypah, Glasshoppah. Take. Take. Take.'

'Thank you, master,' Sammy said as he went out and didn't look back to see the man staring after him.

Sammy crossed the street and sat on a bench to contemplate the incredibility of the world. He looked at the building he had just come out of. It was an ugly Victorian building fairly liberally encrusted with birdshit. Where did it get the idea that it was a Temple? Strange were the ways of the world.

An old man came and sat on the bench beside Sammy. His clothes looked as if they had been put through a mangle with him in them. His face was blotched and lumpy and his skin sagged enough to have been someone else's he had just borrowed for a time. Sammy wondered what his story was. Perhaps he was one of those who at seventeen had filled in the kind of form Sammy had in his hand. Perhaps he had filled in the form and then opted out too late to find anything else he wanted to do and now just wandered around, trying to find out who he was. When he was younger, he probably looked a bit like Robert Duvall. Sammy had seen Robert Duvall in a picture called *Tender Mercies*. It was a good picture. Robert Duvall was a Country and Western singer whose career had been ruined by alcoholism. Sammy liked Country and Western. He didn't *like* it exactly. He was more amazed by it. It was so full of outrageous feelings, it answered something in himself. The old man saw Sammy looking at him and started to sing. His voice was reedy and it quavered a lot but you could tell he meant it.

'When you live in a bottle, it's board and it's bed.
You pull the warm whisky right over your head.
It's sister, it's brother, it's father and mother.
It's all the old friends who are dead.
I just need a little to get me a bottle
And I'll have a warm place I can lie.
With luck it's the one where I'll die.

See, I wasn't bad, was a bit of a lad
And wanted the things that I'd never had.
But they're selling life here
At a price that's too dear.
I'm a fool and I answered the ad,
Again and again and again
And I've lived in a bottle since then.

Hey, don't you be afraid.
This face that I've made
Is less ugly than what I have seen
It's a map of old pain
Where I'm going again.
It's just all the places I've been.

Five pence would be aces
To keep me from places
I feel myself going again.
And I've lived in a bottle since then.'

The old man was starting back on the opening chorus
when Sammy gave him the ten pence.

'God bless ye, son,' the old man said. 'Ye wouldn't have
a fag on ye?'

It occurred to Sammy that it was a good thing they weren't
in America. Words meant different things in different places.
He knew a lot about America. Some day he hoped to go there.
Sammy smoked very little and he wasn't sure if he had any
cigarettes. But he found a packet with two in it and they took
one each. Then Sammy located a match in the ticket pocket
of his jacket and picked the fluff off it and struck it on the metal
of the bench and they shared the light.

'You're all right,' the old man said as if he were bestowing
a knighthood.

Sammy wanted to give him more but he needed the
money for betting. They said cheerio and Sammy crossed
the street, crumpling the application form as he went.

Outside the door of the building he had been in, he put his cigarette to the fuse of the old-fashioned anarchist's bomb in his hand and threw it into the entrance hall of the building. He heard the tremendous explosion as he walked along the street but didn't look back.

Sammy spent two hours in the bookmaker's. While he was there, he saw a few people he knew. Spartacus had turned up. Having seen him before, Sammy recognised him at once. He liked to vary his appearance, being in hiding. Today he was wearing jeans and a jerkin and polo-neck. He could have been anybody but the strength of the eyes was unmistakable, that sense that the second insurrection could take place any time. He was just waiting for the sign. Wat Tyler was with him. There was an anonymous creep who seemed to be watching them. But it was the talent of people like him to be anonymous.

Sammy's system worked today. He restricted himself to races where there were enough horses running to give him an each way bet. Having isolated those races, he concentrated on horses that were neither first or second favourites nor rank outsiders. Within that restricted range he made his choice on the basis of recent form, trainer and jockey. That way, in spite of the small amounts of money he was putting on, a win would mean quite a few pounds and often enough a place got him his money back. He came out winning twenty-two pounds. He could give his mother something and still have more betting money, besides the cache of eight fivers he had in his bedroom. He decided he was quite well off.

Sammy walked. The travelogue didn't happen today. Many times when he was walking around the town there would be a commentary on what he was seeing. The voice varied. Sometimes it was mock American, sometimes fruitily English, sometimes heavily metallic as if it came from another planet. But today there was just the grey town with a hint of rain in the clouds.

He reached the pub just after six. Pauline was due in at quarter past. He wasn't seeing her for long. She was baby-sitting tonight from seven o'clock onwards. He could have gone with her but she was taking her young sister along and being with Pauline and Denise together was for Sammy like having an erection with a padlock on it. The more excited you got, the more painful it felt. Otherwise, baby-sitting would have been a good idea.

Sammy and Pauline had made a kind of love already but it hadn't felt like anything Sammy had read about. Sammy blamed the fact that they had only done it outdoors. Once had been in the shadows at the back of a tenement and an old woman came out to put out the rubbish and seemed to forget what she had come for. While she hovered around as if she couldn't remember her way back home, Sammy and Pauline had stood frozen. Sammy had stared embarrassedly at the wall, as if he had accidentally left something inside Pauline and he didn't know how to ask for it back. Luckily, the old woman's eyesight hadn't been good. But that was no way to discover the mind-blowing effects of passion. They must find a bed, Sammy had decided.

In a bed, you could take your time, explore each other. You wouldn't have to keep turning your head, like a lighthouse to see where the danger was. You could take as long as you liked and, when it was over, you could talk or smoke and maybe even do it again. That should be possible. Danny McLintock had bragged about doing it ten times in the one night. Sammy knew that was ridiculous. But twice should be possible. But they would need a bed. Baby-sitting would give them one.

He bought a half-pint of lager. He didn't drink much since the time he had taken the nine pints of lager and two vodkas and tried to climb the oldest church in the town. He had sprained his ankle and had had to hide in the graveyard when two policemen arrived. The carved, chipped name, 'John Inglis', had stared out at him like a warning. It was the same with pot. He had tried it three times. Once he couldn't stop giggling. Twice he was sick. He had wanted to try it after reading *The Doors of Perception* by Aldous Huxley. But the only door it had ever shown him was the lavatory door. Sammy decided he knew what was wrong. His mind was still too volatile. Introduce much alcohol or drugs and it went into outer space. He would try again when he was older.

This wasn't like an ordinary pub. It was more like a bistro which, Sammy slowly realised as he sat in it, was in Paris, quite close to 'Les Deux Magots'. Sammy knew a lot about Paris. Some day he hoped to go there. An elderly man and woman sat at a table in a corner, saying nothing to each other. They were brooding on the nature of age and going over Yeats's *Byzantium* in their minds. Two tousled young men were talking out of earshot. Sammy doubted if they would ever resolve the question of free choice in a society founded upon economic inequality but he admired the intensity of their commitment. Sammy sipped his lager slowly and thoughtfully but Albert Camus, probably Sammy's all-time favourite intelligence, didn't come in. If he had, Sammy was ready to discuss with him *The Rebel*, the book which, more than any other, had taken possession of his mind.

But Pauline came in. They talked about various things but Pauline had no way of avoiding taking Denise with her when she was baby-sitting. Sammy was intrigued by how changeable Pauline's face was. She had come in looking a little like Audrey Hepburn in *Roman Holiday* and by the time they parted she was reminding him of Sigourney Weaver in *Ghostbusters*.

Sammy walked. Sammy liked walking. In some ways he loved this old grotty town. Dingy though it was, especially in the rain and it rained often enough, it wound itself round your bones. It was the people, Sammy decided. He liked the people. Take his parents. It was easy to love his mother.

She was kind far beyond any kindness life showed her in return. But even his father he found no difficulty in loving, his father who sometimes appeared to have taken a degree in grumpiness. There was a defiant, last-hopeless-stand quality to his father that Sammy appreciated, a trapped animal pretending it isn't afraid. His father was all right.

Most of the people around him were. It was the circumstances of their lives that Sammy rebelled against, the greyness, the lack of horizons, the acceptance of whatever was given. Walking through the dull streets, Sammy became for ten minutes a revolutionary. El Nelsono would lead his people to freedom. Posters would appear everywhere: forty million pesetas for the head of Nelsono. But no one would betray him. Viva Nelsono!

The vision dispersed, leaving the houses with the lights in the rooms where people were watching television and waiting for whatever would happen to come to them. Sammy liked people too much to be a revolutionary. He wasn't a revolutionary, he was a poet.

He was a poet, transforming life into bright colours wherever he touched it. He walked the streets for more than an hour-and-a-half, being a poet. The rain helped. As he gazed at the lighted windows, dramatic clusters of words formed in his mind, dissolving almost as soon as they had shaped themselves.

The window is a picture-frame
Where horror sits without a name.
You only say what you have said.
The child is weeping and you smile.
The corpse is laid out on your bed.
The ruin goes for mile on mile.

Here from dishevelled vagrancy,
The bloodshot words and unkempt deeds,
The white nights and black mornings,

The wanderings through folds of skin,
This endless storm I'm houseless in,
I see you and shout warnings.

The book is blank, the picture's fake,
The worm is in the wedding cake,
The teapot mashes arsenic.

There was more but nobody heard him and it was exhausting being a poet and Sammy went home. His mother wasn't in. It was her night for going to the Labour Club with Mrs Carlin. His father had succumbed to the effect of coming off the nightshift. He was asleep on the couch with the television on. Three empty lager cans lay on the floor beside him.

It occurred to Sammy that his parents wouldn't expect to hear the result of his interview for a week or two. They knew there would be a lot of people in for the job. All they would do at this stage would be to ask Sammy how the interview had gone, his mother anxious, his father quizzing him like a policeman, wondering what social crime he had committed this time. That gave Sammy a problem. Should he let them enjoy for a week or so the possibility at last of his being something other than a misfit? Or would that be more cruel than just telling them outright that he wasn't being considered for the job? He would decide in the morning.

He was tired. Other people might have felt it was a quiet day but, as far as he was concerned, quite a lot had happened. He hung his jacket over a chair and sat looking at the television his father had left on. The Prime Minister was talking to an interviewer, or rather she was bouncing long monologues off an interviewer who was bland enough to stand in for a wall. Sammy didn't like her.

'Of course, we must realise,' the Prime Minister was saying, as if the nation were a kindergarten school. 'We must realise that the world doesn't owe us a living. We must work for it.' Maybe she had been listening to Sammy's guru. 'Each person must take responsibility for his or her own life. It is the achievement of this government to create the climate where that is possible. Our record is second to none in that respect.'

'Crap!' Sammy said to the television.

The Prime Minister faltered. Her eyes looked shiftily at Sammy and she paused.

'Of course,' she resumed, 'this is a lot of nonsense and I might as well tell you the truth. The achievements I've been boasting of don't really exist. What my government has really done is try to dismantle generations of progress in our society. We have created mass unemployment. We have made the rich richer and the poor poorer. We have created a divided nation. We have made the old miserable and the young hopeless. Our record is utterly abominable and if you had any sense you wouldn't vote for us again.'

Sammy nodded and crossed and turned the television off. His father was still asleep on the couch.

'Papa,' Sammy said to him. 'I've decided not to accept my inheritance. No, no. I must insist. I know my behaviour must seem devilish impractical to you. But I have made my decision. I shall be a modern knight errant. I know it's dangerous. But what the devil. With the trusty lance of my imagination, I shall challenge the dragons of our time. Pray for me, Papa. Pray that I don't fall victim to any of the monsters of boredom or indifference or acceptance of pomposity or belief in lies.'

Sammy's father turned over on the couch and started to snore in a different key.

'I'll leave you now,' Sammy said. 'I fear my decision has rendered you speechless. There is a sadness in this farewell. For who knows who I shall be tomorrow? Who knows who we shall all be? Eh, Papa? Goodbye then. And try to remember. You're not really losing a son. You're gaining a new world.'

Sammy's father hadn't stirred. He didn't stir when Sammy went out and went upstairs. It was almost forty minutes before he coughed and snuffled himself awake. He had a mouth like a badger's bum. Life tasted rancid.

He swung his stockinged feet on to the floor and stared at nothing. One thought floated to the surface of his mind like a dead fish belly-up. Mary wasn't in yet. He might as well wait for her in bed. He went through to the kitchen and put the empty lager cans in the bin. As he came upstairs, he noticed the light on in Sammy's room. He looked in to warn Sammy yet again about the damage to your eyes that was caused by reading.

But Sammy was asleep. He lay with a paperback book open on his chest and around him the room was like a bunker fortified with books and records and prints and posters.

He was dreaming.